CW00394894

NO DIRECTION HOME

ORDINARY PEOPLE SURVIVNG
EXTRAORDINARY TIMES

BOOK 1

MIKE SHERIDAN

Editing by Felicia Sullivan

Proofreading by Laurel Kriegler

Cover art by Deranged Doctor Design

CHAPTER 1

Three days after the first case of vPox was reported in Knoxville, Cody Parsons's two roommates, Joe Frisch and Chrissie Sabatini, took ill. Joe showed the symptoms first. He ran a high temperature and complained of a splitting headache. The following day, the first signs of lesions appeared: blotchy red patches that covered his body and soon became pus-filled.

There was a look of alarm on Chrissie's face when he pulled up his T-shirt to show them. They stretched across his entire stomach and chest. Some of them had burst and oozed a thick yellowish liquid.

She recoiled in horror, staggered back several feet and put her hand to her mouth. "My God!" she gasped. "That's horrible!"

"Do they hurt?" Cody asked, still staring at the pustules as Joe pulled down his shirt. Instantly, he regretted such a stupid question. Joe had obviously been scratching at them like crazy.

"They itch like hell, but it's the headache that's the worst part," Joe replied, his voice weak. "This must be that *flu* thing they've been talking about on TV."

For the past few days, the news stations had been reporting on a mysterious illness sweeping the nation, a bad flu, they called it. They'd kept details vague, stating that there had only been a few isolated deaths, mainly among the very young and the elderly.

The Internet and social media hadn't been quite so circumspect, however. Chatter was rife about a lethal viral agent having been released from a biological warfare lab. By who, exactly, no one knew, but there was plenty of speculation: it was the work of Islamic terrorists, the Russians, the Chinese, a US rogue agent. The list was endless.

Cody had seen some horrific-looking photos on his FB newsfeed too, that got quickly taken down. They had to be fake—no real person could ever look that bad. One thing was sure though: once it hit town, the rate of infection was alarming. A few days after it reached Knoxville, it became common to see people with blotchy faces on the streets, some clutching feebly to lampposts and handrails.

Joe stared at Cody, his eyes strained and unfocused. "Can you take me to the hospital?" he asked. "I don't think I can make it on my own."

Natural survival instincts kicked in. *Not in a million years*, they screamed at Cody hysterically. He calmed them down. It was June, college had just ended. For the past week, he and Joe had been drinking beer and eating the same snacks as they sat together on the couch, high-fiving when the contestant of some stupid TV reality show got kicked off. It was too late to avoid this thing now.

"Sure," he said. "We better get you down there right away, see if they can fix you up with some medicine."

Looking around, he saw that Chrissie had gone to her room. It didn't surprise him; she wasn't exactly the caring sort. Cody had quickly learned that you don't really get to know a person until you share a house with them. Though, if he was honest, in this case, he couldn't blame her.

The three attended the University of Tennessee, Knoxville. Like Cody, both Joe and Chrissie wanted a certain independence from the college and chose to live off campus, and although Cody was born and raised in Knoxville, three years ago his mother had sold the family home and relocated to Phoenix, taking Simon, Cody's younger brother, with her. It was the reason he had to rent.

Neither of the three came from wealthy families, and they lived in a cheap three-bedroom house in the northwest of the city, just off I-75. It wasn't exactly the greatest of locations, but the highway ran south all the way downtown, and it didn't take them long to get to their classes.

Cody's mom was paying his college fees, though he took as much of the burden off her as he could with an endless series of jobs. During his three years at UTK, he'd worked as a caddy, a barista, a baker, then, his last job, as a lab technician at an optical firm. That had turned out pretty well. The company was in the process of dropping the Oakley brand, and he'd been able to buy a few hundred sunglasses cheap and sell them on Ebay. Not coming from money meant he'd learned how to hustle from an early age.

Grabbing his jacket, he took Joe outside and bundled him into the back of his old Subaru Legacy, then drove to the Physicians Regional Medical Center in North Knoxville, the nearest hospital to where they lived.

Twenty minutes later, he parked outside the emergency department, relieved to see there weren't many cars in the lot. Hopefully it meant they wouldn't have to wait long for Joe to get seen.

Unfortunately, there was a reason for the lack of vehicles. Crossing the lot, Cody spotted two soldiers dressed in digital-gray combat uniforms guarding the entrance, semi-automatic rifles slung over their shoulders. M16s. Cody's father had served in Iraq, and had taught him how to identify weapons when he was still a boy.

One of the men, a large black soldier, began to wave them away before they'd even reached the doorway. "Hospital is full. No new patients being admitted," he told them in a flat tone that said he'd been doing this all day.

"My friend is seriously ill," Cody said. "Can't you make an exception?"

The soldier shook his head. "Your friend is no exception. The whole town is sick. Even me. I've had a splitting headache all morning and they haven't even given me as much as a goddamn aspirin."

Cody stared closer at the soldier and could see a clammy sheen on his face, his skin ash gray.

"Which base are you guys from?" he asked, naturally curious about all military matters. His father had been stationed at nearby Fort Campbell, Kentucky, home to the 101st Airborne and the 5th Special Forces Group. His father had been in the 5th SFG, something Cody was particularly proud of.

"McGhee Tyson," the soldier replied. "We're National Guard. Didn't you hear? Governor Dickinson declared a state of emergency this morning."

Cody's eyes widened. "State of emergency? Why, because of this flu thing?"

"That's it, bud," said the second soldier. He sounded a little friendlier than his companion. "Except it ain't no flu. It's some type of damned pox. People are coming down like flies with it. It's how come we can't let any more patients in. Come back tomorrow morning, but you better get here early if you want any chance of him being admitted."

Cody stared at him in alarm. "Really? How serious is this?"

The soldier shrugged. "Serious enough for the president to be making an address on television soon. Other than that, I couldn't tell you." He grinned. "It's not like me and George are on the Joint Chiefs of Staff or something. They told us to haul our asses down here, so that's what we did."

Cody thanked the soldier, then helped Joe back to the car. By now, he was considerably weaker than when they'd first left the house. Simply walking fifty yards seemed to have expended all his energy.

They drove to two other hospitals, Fort Sanders and East Tennessee Baptist. It was the same situation at both of them. After that, there was no choice but to go home. By then, Joe was in terrible shape. Cody had to stop the car twice so he could vomit on the street. The third time, Joe didn't warn him. Turning around to the sound of gagging, Cody saw that he was barely conscious. Vomit drooled down his chin and onto the car seat.

Back at the house, he dragged Joe out of the car and put his arm around his waist to get him up the porch steps and through the front door. He arrived in the living room to see Chrissie curled up on couch. She was shivering, her face sweaty and her eyes glassy.

"Go to your room, Chrissie," he told her as he passed her on the way to Joe's room.

"Why? So you don't have to deal with me, is that it?" she called out behind him plaintively.

"No, because you'll be more comfortable." Though if Cody would have admitted it, there was a certain truth to what she said.

Although a humid summer day, as soon as he dropped Joe on the bed, he immediately crawled under the covers and drew himself up into the fetal position.

Cody leaned over him. "Can I get you anything, buddy?" he asked. He'd known Joe almost three years. It hurt him to see him this way.

Joe shook his head. Looking up at him, there was clarity in his eyes for one brief moment. "Thanks, Cody," he whispered. "You're a good friend."

The look of pain and exhaustion returned and Joe turned his head away. Although Cody didn't know it then, they would be the last words Joe spoke to him.

Chrissie had done what he'd asked and gone to her room, he discovered, when he returned to the living room. He went into the kitchen and grabbed the last can of beer from the fridge. Cracking it open, he sat down on the sofa. Other than for fear, stress, and worry, he felt absolutely fine.

CHAPTER 2

"Ah, *jaysus*, this is woeful. I mean absolutely bleedin' brutal."
    Brendan "Jonah" Murphy sat up in bed in his room at the Sun Ray, a small hotel in southwest Orlando. It was not exactly an upmarket location. Then again, hailing from the Oliver Bond Street flats in inner city Dublin, Jonah wasn't exactly an upmarket kind of guy.
    The "flats" were the Irish equivalent to what Americans call the "projects". An Internet property search for Dublin City using keywords such as *upmarket, salubrious,* or *luxurious* would be unlikely to display Jonah's abode on the first zillion pages. Notwithstanding that, to put it in realtor parlance, they were, however, *charmly situated.* Oliver Bond Street was plonk in the city center, a stone's throw away from the Guinness factory, Temple Bar, and a host of other top tourist spots.
    "Primo location, headerball. Yeh couldn't buy that view for a million dollars," Jonah liked to boast anytime anyone asked him where he was from.
    He was in no doubt however, that someday the flats would be bulldozed, to be replaced by high-end developments such as the ones they'd already built down the IFSC, the Irish Financial Services Center, when the Sheriff Street flats had been torn down. Not in his lifetime, he

11

prayed. Born and raised in The Bond, he didn't fancy being relocated to one of the soulless social housing areas outside of the city. He shuddered at the thought.

Sitting in bed beside him was his wife, Colleen. The pair were on their dream vacation in Florida, one they'd scrimped and saved for all year. Since arriving five days ago, they'd done SeaWorld, Universal Studios, and only that afternoon had returned from Disney World.

Tomorrow was the Kennedy Space Center, then the following day, the thing Jonah most looked forward to: a deep-sea fishing trip around Cape Canaveral. Jonah was simply gaga about fishing. Seas, rivers, lakes—he loved them all. Ireland had some of the best fishing locations in the world and he'd been to just about all of them, but tomorrow was *big game* fishing, where he hoped to catch the hugest fish of his life.

For Jonah, reeling in a blue marlin was like a surfer catching the big kahuna, or a Buddhist monk reaching nirvana, only a lot less dignified. There was sure to be a whole lot of whooping and yelling with a bunch of cuss words thrown in for good measure.

Something at the back of his mind was worrying him, however. Something he hoped wasn't going to spoil his big day out. The *brutal* he'd referred to was not the basic facilities of their dank hotel room, or the size of the tiny TV bolted to the wall in the corner. Nor was it even the stale odor that wafted up from the dark-brown carpet, which Colleen had wrinkled up her nose at when they were first shown to their room.

"Don't worry, love," he'd reassured her at the time. "Once we crack open a few beers, the smell will be gone in a jiffy."

No, the *brutal* Jonah referred to was the constant sound of people moaning on either side of them through the wafer-thin walls. They'd heard them from the moment they arrived. Then later that evening, out on the street, the couple saw several people with blotchy faces and nasty looking rashes on their arms and legs. It had been noticeable enough for them to comment on it.

Since then, things had only gotten worse. Just that afternoon at Disney World, even some of the staff had come down with whatever was going around. One of them literally collapsed right in front of them as they'd strolled through the park.

Jonah, being the good-natured bloke that he was, had rushed over, picked him up, and taken him over to the first aid center at the back of Casey's Corner where the couple had stopped earlier for hot dogs and fries. There, they had been shocked to see a line out the door of similarly unwell people.

When they were leaving the park an hour later, Jonah had said to Colleen, "*Jaysus*, love, never in me life did I imagine I'd be traipsing around the Magic Kingdom with Donald bleedin' Duck slung over me shoulder. Yeh don't get a chance like that too often in your life, do you?" He chuckled. "Now yer sure yeh snapped that with the iPhone, aren't yeh?"

Laughing, Colleen had assured him it was all on digital record.

"Great. That'll be on me Facebuke tonight."

Jonah took a sip from his glass of whiskey on the nightstand, his first of the evening. It was 8 p.m. and he didn't usually get into the hard stuff until then. Colleen didn't approve. As for beer? Well, he *was* on holiday, after all.

He glanced over at his wife. "Did yeh hear what I said, love? All this wailing and moaning. It's driving me demented."

There came no reply. Since returning to the hotel, Colleen had been ignoring him, far too absorbed in reading the Kindle he'd bought her a few Christmases ago. Worst present he'd ever gotten her. Since then, she'd been addicted to the damned thing, reading two or three books every week. Some girls spent their money on clothes and makeup, fashion accoutrements and the likes. Not his Colleen. No, she bought eBooks. Now, in the evenings, he could barely get a word out of her. Her beak was always jammed into the piece of plastic, giving him the deaf ear. It drove him potty.

"I may as well be talking to the wall," he grumbled to himself disconsolately.

Colleen didn't read romance either. She was into that post-apocalyptic nonsense that was all the rage these days. He couldn't remember how many times she'd finished a book to excitedly explain to him how the world was going to come to an end soon by a multitude of different means that left him dizzy: pandemics, zombie mutant viruses, nuclear war, solar flares, an EMP strike (whatever the hell that was). The list went on and on.

Jonah couldn't understand what fascinated his wife with all this doom and gloom stuff. He was a simple man, a pint of plain down his local pub, a chat about the footie or the boxing, even the golf – which he wasn't that pushed about, except the Ryder Cup when the Europeans usually gave the Yanks a good thrashing. That was more his thing. But the bleedin' apocalypse? That was just downright depressing.

He took a long sip from his can of beer and put it down next to his whiskey glass again. Another cacophony of moans and wails started up to either side of him. He was getting it in stereo now!

Jonah blew up. He couldn't help himself. Balling up his fist, he banged the wall behind him several times. "Would yis ever shuuuurruup!" he yelled. "*Jaysus,* between the missus not talking to me, and youse lot coughing yer guts up, yis are driving me to distraction!"

Beside him, Colleen dropped her Kindle on her lap. She stared at him incredulously, a deep frown on her face. "Jonah Murphy! Are you out of your mind? Cut that out right now!"

A sheepish grin came over Jonah's ruddy features. "Finally, a bit of attention. Please love, talk to me, I'm bored off me rocker. The neighbors are huffin' and puffin' the walls down, and there you are, gawking at a piece of plastic." He broke out into song. *"Baby, baby, where did our love go?"*

Colleen placed the Kindle down carefully on the nightstand, then picked up her iPad instead. Flicking it open, she said, "All right, Jonah, let's talk. How about something serious this time? Something I've been reading about on the blogs."

Jonah made a face. "Ah, no love. Not the blogs. Not one of these post…ah…ah…apocrofrictical talks. I'm not in the mood tonight. We're on our holliers. I was thinking more along the lines of a kiss and a cuddle, followed up by a little hootchie cootchie."

"Jonah…"

Recently, Colleen had gotten big into the blogs too, soaking up all this weirdo conspiracy stuff. A bunch of bleedin' nutters, in his opinion. Even worse than the books. Lunatics spouting out all these letters that supposedly meant something. SHITFIT. TEOWACKOFF. BUG, BOL and BOB, whoever those clowns were.

Since then, she'd gotten into the habit of asking him kooky questions about how didn't he think it weird that the government did *this* thing or *that* thing, and how come mainstream media supported *this* person or *that* person, but never *this other* person.

"Because *this other* person is someone no one's ever heard of, that's why. Nobody cares what he thinks," he'd tell her. To which Colleen would nod her head vigorously. "Exactly. Because MSM won't give him any coverage, that's why. He's being censored."

I mean, how could you win an argument like that? He'd never even heard of the *Evening Herald* or the *Independent* ever being termed MSM before, although the Indo had a great sports section, he'd say that for them.

Truth be told, though he would never admit it to her, Jonah always enjoyed their talks. A *prepocalypse natter*, he liked to call them. After appeasing Colleen with his thoughts on various doomsday matters, she in turn would appease his more base desires. It was a strange form of foreplay, he often thought to himself. Still, it worked, and Jonah was a practical man. Especially when it came to his nookie.

"Ah, go on then," he sighed. "What's on yer mind this time?"

Colleen took a deep breath and collected her thoughts. She was good at that. She worked as a cashier at the Irish Life insurance company on Abbey Street, and was great with figures. Had a hell of a figure herself, he liked to joke.

"First thing…remember the Ebola scare a while back?"

Jonah nodded. "Yeah, I remember them Ebola mutant zombie books you started reading right about then. Next question?"

"Remember how you couldn't put on the telly without hearing all about it?"

"Yep. That's how come I remember, baby."

"Well then, how come no one is talking this time about the virus that's going around? I mean, they're talking about it, but they're being real vague, and always reassuring everyone that everything is just fine. They didn't do that with Ebola. It was like they were trying to scare everyone to death. Don't you think it's a little strange?"

Jonah shook his head. "No, I don't. Because this is only a flu. Nobody is dying of it. That's why."

Colleen stared at him. "How do you know?"

"Because if they were dying, it would be on the news," Jonah explained patiently. "They wouldn't bleedin' stop talking about it. Just like the last time."

"Em, yeah…unless, of course, it was so serious a disease, they've been ordered *not* to talk about it. Maybe the government wants to keep this thing under cover as long as they can. The last thing they need is panic on the streets while they're making their plans."

Jonah frowned, putting the best *I'm intrigued* expression on his face he could muster. He knew where Colleen was going with this. "You think so? Or maybe it's them New World Order geezers looking to depopulate the world. Could even be the Council for Foreign Relationships." He knew how hot this topic always got her.

"Relations," Colleen corrected him. "The CFR."

Jonah took another sip from his whiskey. "Yeah, them lot. Shower of feckers."

"On the blogs, they say that the hospitals are full around the country," Colleen continued. "People are dying like flies, but no one is talking about it."

"And you believe them…the blogs?" Jonah couldn't help but let a skeptical tone enter his voice.

"Yes, I do. Remember at the park today? The queue out the door of the infirmary?"

Jonah nodded uneasily. Colleen was onto something there. Something he'd put out of his mind. Because right at the very back of it flashed a big red warning sign that read: *Sorry headerball, your fishing trip's been canceled.*

He wasn't having that.

"Another thing. How are you feeling?"

Jonah shrugged. "Not a bother. I'm right as rain." He reached over and picked up his glass of whiskey. "This here's been keeping the bugs away."

Colleen looked at him exasperatedly. "Jonah, seriously, Dr. Arthur Bradley says that even with a laboratory-created killer viral agent, there is always a certain percentage of the population that is immune to it. Think about it. Since we've been here, we've already been exposed to several people who've come down with this thing."

"True enough. Even Donald Duck."

Colleen giggled. "Yes, including Donald Duck. Yet here we are, both right as rain, as you say."

Jonah frowned. "So you and me, we're immune to this thing. That what you're saying?"

"Maybe. From what I've read, the incubation period is short. After three days, people generally start to show signs of infection."

"Then how come neither of us have it? I mean, you'd think that one of us would have caught it by now."

Colleen shrugged. "A statistical anomaly, that's all. It really depends on what percentage of people are immune to it."

From her tone, Jonah guessed his wife wasn't entirely serious about all this. It was merely a bit of nonsense to keep them amused. The world wasn't really about to end. At least, not until after his fishing trip.

"Statistical anomaly, huh?" he said, a gleam in his eye. Between the whiskey and the pink negligee his wife wore, he was starting to feel aroused. Though barely five feet tall, Colleen had serious curves, and with slender legs and ash blonde hair, she turned heads most days of the week. Just then, he remembered that he'd persuaded her to bring a pair of matching high heels for the negligee. He wondered what it would take to get her into them tonight.

"Fascinating, Dr. Murphy. Pray, continue," he said in his most authoritative voice. "I must warn you though, I'll need to conduct a physical examination of you later. Orders from the CDC. There's a couple of 'statistical anomalies' I have to investigate. To be honest, I can barely keep me eyes off them."

CHAPTER 3

Two days later, Cody went into Joe's room to discover he'd passed away. The previous day he'd checked up on him regularly. All that time, he'd remained asleep, although Cody suspected it was a coma, as it had been impossible to wake him. He guessed Joe had died during the night, because at 9 a.m. his body was already stiff.

Chrissie followed soon after and died that afternoon. By the time of their deaths, both were unrecognizable. Festering sores covered their entire faces to the point their features were almost indistinguishable. Falling into comas had been a mercy for them.

What occurred on Inskip Drive, Knoxville, Tennessee, was merely a snapshot of what was happening across the country, perhaps the entire world. When Cody had called his mother the previous day, she was running a high fever, as was his younger brother Simon. That morning they'd stopped answering their phones. Seeing the ravaged bodies of his two roommates, Cody knew with certainty they were dead or dying. When his mother first told him they were sick, he'd offered to drive down to Phoenix, but she'd insisted he stayed where he was. It was a long way from Knoxville to Phoenix. Still, Cody felt guilty as hell.

There was no longer any official denial about the virus, and panic had set in. From what he'd learned from TV and social media, vPox, as it became universally known, acted incredibly swiftly. The incubation period was around three days before symptoms appeared. A few days later, the person was dead. A small percentage of the population was immune to the disease, however, for reasons no one had figured out. Staring at his face in the bathroom mirror, not a blemish to be seen, Cody knew he must be one of them.

Since Chrissie died, other than for state and FEMA sponsored posts, there wasn't much else going on his FB newsfeed. Earlier that day he'd been in contact with some friends at UTK, many of whom weren't sure if they were immune to the disease or not, and had barricaded themselves in their homes. Now, no one responded to his messages or answered their cell phones, and he suspected neither were functional any more.

It felt creepy in the house with two dead bodies lying in their beds. Cody knew he wouldn't be able to sleep that night unless he gave them a proper burial, so that afternoon he started the job.

The house had a scruffy garden at the front and a tiny paved yard out the back, where there was a small shed containing a few gardening tools. Unlocking the padlock to the shed door, Cody grabbed a spade and got to work.

The ground in the front garden was hard, and it took him the best part of three hours to dig a trench long enough to lay both bodies head to toe. It was a blue-skied summer's day, and by the time the grave was ready, his entire t-shirt was soaked with sweat.

Going back into the house, he wrapped Joe up in a thick blanket and brought him out over his shoulder. It was the first time in his life Cody had ever touched a dead body. Rigor mortis had fully set in and it felt like he was carrying a bag of cement, not a friend he'd grown close to these past three years.

He wrapped Chrissie up in another blanket. Her body was still soft, and he carried her out in his arms like she was a sleeping child and laid her down beside Joe. Picking up the spade, he shoveled the earth over them until he'd refilled the trench.

After that, he tore down some of the wooden siding from the porch, made two simple crosses, and stuck them into the dirt to either end of the trench. Stooping his head, he placed his hands together and mumbled a few words. He barely knew what he was saying, though he was conscious of using the word *God* several times. It was the best he could do.

Once he was done, Cody sat down on the sofa and buried his head in his hands. A feeling of total loneliness overwhelmed him. He struggled to make sense of things, and had to fight hard to stop panic from setting in. Everything had happened so fast, his mind could barely take it all in.

It was then that the lights went out.

It was summertime, 6 p.m. The curtains were pushed back, and he could still see from the natural light outside. Nonetheless, it gave him a start. He picked up the TV's remote and tried switching it on. Nothing. He stood up and hit every light switch on the wall, then went over to the refrigerator in the kitchen, hitting the switch on the way too. Everything was dead.

Then it dawned on him. Something he'd given no consideration to until now. The nation's power grid wasn't something that ran in the background without human attendance, or at least, not for very long. Without anyone to feed the systems, they would eventually shut down. It appeared that moment had arrived.

Another thought occurred to him. He ran into the bathroom and turned on the faucet. Clear water ran out of it. Relieved, he filled up the sink and every other empty container he could find, including the green recycling cart outside. Who knew when the water would run out.

When he was done, he went into his room. Reaching under the bed, he pulled out a shoebox where he stored the few personal possessions he owned. Inside were some photos of Cody and his father dating back to when he was a teenager. They were from around the time his parents had split up.

Also inside was the Kimber 1911 .45 pistol his father had willed to him when he died. He took it out, grabbed his denim jacket, and headed out of the house. Having been cooped up for the last few days with two dying persons, Cody needed to get out and search for other survivors. Healthy people. Just like him.

CHAPTER 4

Dusk was approaching as Cody headed east on Inskip to pick up the I-75. Looking down at the Subaru's fuel gauge, he saw it was less than a quarter full. He hadn't refilled it on his way back from the hospital the other day, and it had already been low then. That was when his second day late and dollar short revelation hit him. Would the stations pump gas without electricity? It was something he hadn't thought of until now. Something told him they wouldn't.

He decided to go to the Chevron Quick Mart on Magnolia Avenue. It was three miles east of downtown, close to his old house before his mother and Simon moved out to Phoenix. Normally, it was a busy station and he thought it might be the kind of place where he'd find people looking to either leave or enter the city.

On the way, other than the occasional abandoned car, he didn't see anyone else on the road, though once off the freeway, he spotted lights behind the curtains of some of the houses. They weren't the normal brightness you'd see from a sixty watt bulb, and he guessed the illumination came from kerosene lamps or candles.

Arriving at the station, his eyes lit up when he saw two cars parked in the forecourt; a red Ford F-150 pickup and a cream colored sedan. He drove by slowly and spotted a

23

heavyset black man and a skinny white guy. They leaned against the pickup drinking beers. Next to the black guy, an assault rifle rested against the hood.

The man waved to Cody as he passed by. A friendly wave. Slowing down, Cody made a U-turn, drove back to the station, and pulled up ten feet away from where the two vehicles were parked. He got out of the Subaru and walked over to the men.

"Hey there, fellah!" the black guy greeted him in a local Tennessee drawl. "Sure is nice to see another survivor." Broad shouldered, showing signs of a paunch under his white T-shirt, he had short-cropped hair flecked with gray and a trimmed goatee that had a little gray in it too. Cody took him to be in his late-forties. The white man, small and wiry, looked about the same age. Smoking a cigarette, he appeared less confident, a little more wary than his companion.

Reaching them, Cody let out a big sigh. "Do you guys have any idea how happy I am to see you?" He shook his head. "Man, I just spent the last two days caring for my two roommates. I buried them both this afternoon."

"How you coping, son?" the black guy asked. Cody could hear real emotion in his voice.

"Haven't really thought about it. Guess I've been too busy doing what I had to do."

"That's a sign right there you're doing good." Tears welled up in the man's eyes. "I put my wife and sixteen-year-old daughter in the ground this morning. Hardest thing I've had to do my entire life."

The white guy grimaced. "That's tough. To be honest, this whole thing hasn't been as hard on me. I hadn't seen my family in over ten years. As for friends, can't say I had too many of them either. Maybe one or two to talk to in a bar every once in a while, that's about it."

"Never thought you'd see the day you'd be thankful for that, did you?" The black guy stuck his hand out toward Cody. "I'm Walter, by the way. This here is Pete."

"Cody." He shook both men's hands, then pointed over to the pumps. "Are they working?" he asked. "I'm running low on fuel. I got about enough to get me home tonight, that's all."

Pete shook his head. "'Fraid not, kid. No power, no pump. No pump, no gas. Simple as that."

"Damn, I should have thought about that sooner. Guess I don't know much about disaster preparedness. At least I remembered to fill up with as much water as I could back at the house, though it took the power cutting off to remind me."

Walter nodded. "It's good you did that right away. The water treatment plants use huge pumps to filter and pressurize the water mains. Once water pressure decreases, you risk contamination from backflow, so don't drink it even if it looks clear—it'll make you sick as a dog. Don't worry about gas though. Tomorrow I'm planning on rigging up a pump system here."

He pointed over to one side of the forecourt. "I've found the refueling ports where the tankers fill up. I'll just drop a hose and pump it right out. In the meantime, you can get gas out of the cars in your neighborhood."

Cody brightened up at that. "Good idea. I never thought about siphoning gas. Of course, I can use my roommates' cars too," he added, suddenly thinking of that.

"Just remember, a lot of cars these days have anti-siphon blocks, but you can drain the fuel from underneath. A plastic pan and screwdriver is all you need for most." Walter shook his head. "Who'd of thought the world would go to hell so fast that stealing gas from your neighbor would be the right thing to do?"

"How come you know so much about all this, Walter?" Pete asked curiously. "Me, I can barely find the fuel cap on my lawn mower. Guess that's what comes of being a bookkeeper your whole life."

It was at that point Cody realized that Walter and Pete had only just met. There had been a certain familiarity in the way the two leaned side by side against the pickup when he'd arrived that had made him think otherwise. Obviously, that was just down to circumstances.

"Seventeen years as a US Army combat engineer learned me stuff," Walter replied with a grin. "Did my fair share of fighting too. Fallujah. Now that was one sonofabitch."

"Really? There were army engineers at Fallujah?" Cody asked. "My father fought there too. He never mentioned anything about that."

Walter looked at him. "Who do you think disabled the power at the substations when the Army and Marines went in that first night? And that was just the start."

"Of course, never thought about that. My father said it was hell. Worse thing he went through his entire time there."

Walter nodded. "It was bad. Still, nothing compared to this."

"I hear you," Pete said, shaking his head. "I still wake up every morning hoping this is just a bad dream."

"Deal with it," Walter advised. "Things ain't going to get better anytime soon. Most likely, they'll get a damned sight worse."

Cody stared at him. "What makes you say that?"

"Nothing like a disaster to turn man back to his natural state," Walter replied. "That's when he becomes an animal. A smart one, but an animal all the same." He glanced at both of them. "You seen any sign of the gangs yet?"

Cody shook my head. "Nope. I haven't been out much though."

"Yeah, I've seen them," Pete said. "There's one around my way already. A group of about seven or eight. Men mainly, though the leader's already got himself a girl." He hesitated a moment. "To be honest, I'm thinking I might join them. Safety in numbers, they say. How about you, Walter? You want I put in a word for you? You too, kid?" he said, turning to Cody.

Cody looked at Walter, waiting for him to respond. Walter shook his head. "Not my style, though I appreciate you asking. There *is* safety in numbers, I grant you, but for that, usually you got to give up the freedom to think for yourself. Gangs run top down, just like the Army. After taking orders for seventeen years, I swore I'd never do it again."

Pete looked disappointed. "I'm not even sure they'll let me join. Not much need for bookkeepers these days. So what's your plan, Walter? You going to keep on living here by yourself?"

"Nope, I plan on leaving the city. Soon as I stock up on everything I need, I'm heading for the hills. I'll hunt and fish, then in a month or so I'll come down and see how things have panned out."

"Wish I knew how to hunt and fish," Pete said wistfully. "I'm not cut out for that sort of thing. To be honest, I've never even tried. Been a pen pusher my whole life."

"It's never too late to learn." Walter turned to Cody. "How about you, kid? You ready for what's coming next?"

"I guess so. My dad taught me how to handle weapons. He lived in Greenville, South Carolina, and used to take me into the Chattahoochee forest regularly. Did plenty of hunting and fishing there. Last time was eight years ago though."

"Don't worry. You'll get into the swing of it again." Walter stared at him. "What happened to your father? Did the pox take him away?"

"No. He died six years ago." Cody hesitated a moment. "Things ended up kind of badly for him."

Walter looked at him sympathetically. "Happened too often to those who served our country. We came back with experiences no one here ever had to deal with. A head full of stuff that don't just disappear *like that*," he said, snapping his fingers. "Everyone back home expected it to, though. That was the thing."

Cody nodded. "That's exactly what happened to my dad. Mom didn't understand him anymore when he got home. They split up a couple of years later. Then things just got worse…"

There was more to the story, but he didn't feel like talking about it. In fact, he was surprised he'd said that much. He hadn't told Joe about what happened until he'd known him for over a year. Even then, it took a night of hard drinking for it to all come out.

"Being a soldier takes its toll on families. I know all about that too," Walter said quietly. "Well guys, you two seem like decent sorts. You're both welcome to come with me when I leave town." He smiled wryly. "Everyone needs a little companionship to stop them going batshit crazy in the boonies."

Cody's eyes lit up. "I'll come. I'd like that. There's nothing to keep me here anymore."

"How about you, Pete?" Walter asked. "You good for that too? Don't worry, I'll teach you how to hunt deer in no time at all."

Pete looked doubtful. "Maybe. I'm not sure if I can hack it in the forest."

"Think about it. I won't be going for a couple more days."

The three talked some more, then a while later called it a night, arranging to meet the next day around 4 p.m. Walter lived close by on Cherry Street, a couple of miles west of the zoo. Pete lived somewhere north of the I-640 loop.

"I don't want to seem inhospitable not inviting you to my home," Walter told the two as they were leaving. "It's just I need to spend some time alone in the house before I go. Say a proper goodbye to my wife and daughter. I hope you both understand."

Cody and Pete had no problem with that. After shaking hands, they all got into their vehicles and left.

Driving home, Cody felt a sense of relief. He was no longer alone in the world. He'd found a friend in Walter, and would leave the city with him once the two had stocked up on supplies. Perhaps Pete would come with them too.

Walter had given him the address of a gun shop to go to the following day. Without the Internet, it would save a lot of driving around. He'd advised Cody to stock up on ammunition for the Kimber, also to pick out a semi-automatic rifle, saying an AR-15 style rifle was best. He was to get plenty of ammo for that too.

Arriving home, Cody felt grateful for one other thing. That he'd buried Joe and Chrissie that afternoon. It would have been hard to return to the house if he hadn't.

CHAPTER 5

In the park close to the Sun Ray Hotel, Jonah Murphy wiped the sweat from his brow. It was midday, the sun scorching, and he felt hot and sticky. His freckled Irish skin was unused to this type of heat, and he felt like a lobster chucked into a pot of boiling water. Still, he was alive and kicking. He and Colleen had survived vPox while a vast amount of the population had not. How many had died exactly, no one was sure.

He took a swig from his tepid can of beer. The electricity had gone off in the hotel that morning, and in the sweltering heat nothing stayed cold for long.

"Yer right, love," he said, turning to Colleen, sitting on the park bench beside him. "Look at us. We really are a couple of statistical anomalies, aren't we?"

Colleen took a sip from her Diet Coke. "I still can't believe it," she said, shaking her head. "It all happened so fast."

The speed of the deadly infection had been incredible. Over the past two days, everywhere the couple had gone there had been people collapsing on the streets, crawling along the sidewalks, retching into trashcans. Horrific pus-filled lumps covered their arms and legs. Their faces became hideously disfigured and blood dripped out of their ears, their noses, even their eyes. Jonah had seen a few zombie movies in his time—it was on that kind of scale. vPox didn't leave any good-looking corpses behind, that was for sure.

Unlike zombies, however, the infected didn't cause any trouble and most died in their homes. After coming down with the initial symptoms, within hours they crawled into their beds, never to rise from them again.

The Sun Ray lay quiet. Since the outbreak, some Americans tourists not yet too weak, had elected to drive back to their homes. Trapped foreigners such as Jonah and Colleen had stayed on, along with the dead and the dying. A middle-aged American woman had remained too. She'd arrived with her husband and two children, but had been the only one to survive. There was also a German man whose wife had died. Both had looked shell-shocked when Jonah spoke briefly to them that morning.

"What I can't understand is how *anyone* survived," Jonah said. "I mean…why us?"

"The most plausible theory I saw on the blogs is that some of us have natural immunity to the disease dating back to the Middle Ages when the Bubonic plague ravaged across Europe."

Jonah stared at Colleen blankly. "Yeh what?"

"A mutation of one of our genes. CCR5 to be specific. Apparently there's a high concentration of the mutation among Eurasians. It may provide resistance to smallpox, including this weaponized variant of it."

Jonah digested all this. "So we're mutants, that it? Does that mean we got special powers too?"

"Jonah, shut up," Colleen snapped. "What are we going to do? How are we going to get home?" she asked, a look of desperation on her face.

Jonah shook his head. "I don't know, love. If I knew how to fly a plane, I'd take yeh home in a 747. Seeing as I can't, it looks like we're stuck here."

Colleen's lower lip trembled. "I'm so worried about Mam and the rest of the family. I-I just hope everything is all right back home, that it's not like here."

The last thing the couple heard before the Internet packed it in was that Ireland had closed its borders, canceling all international flights and ferries. Jonah prayed that the government had reacted in time. Dublin was a busy European city. People traveled to the country from all over the world, including several daily US flights. It only took one infected person to arrive and Ireland would suffer the same fate as America.

"She'll be fine. So will the rest of your family. Mine too," he said comfortingly. While they didn't have any children of their own yet, both he and his wife came from large families.

Colleen caught hold of her emotions. "Jonah, we need to start making plans. We can't stay in the hotel forever. We need to move soon."

Jonah nodded. "The bodies, right? With the aircon off, they're going to start stinking."

"It's not just that. Once the food disappears from the supermarket shelves, there'll be no way to survive here in the city."

Jonah hadn't thought of that. "What about the government? Don't tell me they won't do anything. Maybe we should just wait until they arrive."

Colleen snorted. "What's left of the government is in an underground bunker right now. They're not helping anyone. Anyway, what do you expect them to do? Fly down and help out stranded tourists in Florida? Even if there is anything left of FEMA, they'll only throw us into a camp. Rations will be scarce, and pretty soon the gangs will take what little we're given."

Jonah stared at her suspiciously. "Who told you that? Dr. Arthur bleedin' Bradley?"

He knew Colleen's reasoning came from those crazy books she read. Still, he had to admit, most of the points she'd made had all been realized so far. It looked like the government had kept this thing under cover as long as they could, preventing panic from spreading while they took care of themselves. Maybe the books weren't as crazy as he'd thought.

Colleen sighed. "No, Jonah. In this case, Franklin *bleedin'* Horton."

"Yeah? And who's he when he's at home?"

"He's a prepper. He knows his stuff. Says we got to figure this out on our own. We got to stock up on food, water, medicine. And guns. Who knows how people are going to behave from here on in?"

"Then what? Head for the hills and put on funny accents?"

Colleen stared at him. "Why on Earth would we put on funny accents?"

"You know, to blend in with the hillbillies. 'Course, as far as everyone here's concerned, we already got funny accents."

Colleen smiled weakly. "That's true. God knows what they'll think of us."

"I'll see if I can snag a banjo somewhere," Jonah mused. "I'm great on the 'ol guitar, I should pick it up quick enough. Maybe try me hand at the claw hammer style, like that Ralph Stanley geezer."

Colleen had put on a serious face again. "Let's walk back up to the supermarket and stock up on more food. We'll load up two trolleys and wheel them back to the hotel. This time we need to get the basics too…salt, sugar, cooking oil. Stuff like that."

With no restaurants open, the couple had been making trips to the Publix supermarket at the top of the Kirkham Road. It was a fifteen minute walk away.

"All right. Then what?"

Colleen hesitated, and Jonah could see her mind whirring busily. "Tonight I'll make a list of everything we need to get. Top priority is guns, medicine, camping supplies, hunting and fishing gear, and proper outdoor clothes."

Jonah's ears pricked up. "Did you say fishing gear?"

Colleen nodded. "Supermarket food won't last forever. Pretty soon, we'll need to find it ourselves."

There was a determined gleam in Jonah's eye. "I'll take care of the fishing and camping gear. I've been on enough fishing trips in me life to know what to bring. You figure out the medicine and the weapons. You've read enough of them prepper bukes to know what to get. I'm from Ireland, what do I know about guns? I'm not a bleedin' bank robber." He cracked a smile. "Though I can't say I didn't think about becoming one back when I didn't have a pot to piss in."

Colleen frowned. "Jonah...*really*?"

"Before I met you, love," Jonah added hastily. "Anyway, I blew the idea off. It's a mug's game. Anyone I know that tried it ended up dead or doing a stretch in The Joy."

Mountjoy, "The Joy," was Dublin's main prison. Due to his upbringing, Jonah had many acquaintances that had done time there.

"Never fancied doing a stretch there. It's not the free bed or the free food I object to, it's the free sex."

When he saw his constant joking wasn't going to cheer his wife up, he drained his beer and stood up. "All right love, let's get cracking. With your brains and my brawn, maybe we'll get through this thing after all."

CHAPTER 6

Ralph "The Face" Chambers rode down Interstate 75, taking an S-bend at ninety miles an hour. Ahead of him, the highway lay empty. Zero traffic. Normally at this hour, Atlanta's Downtown Connector was chock-a-bloc, one of the most congested highways in the United States. Not anymore. That was just fine with Ralph.

He rode a brand new Harley CVO Breakout, a semi-automatic rifle strapped across his back. A week ago, the Harley had a price tag of twenty-five thousand dollars. That morning he'd picked it up for nothing. Breaking into the showroom on Thornton Road, he'd selected his machine of choice. Shortly after that, he figured out where management kept the keys.

Next stop had been a gun store, where he'd seized a Bushmaster AR 15, picking up plenty of ammunition for it too, along with a bunch of nine millimeter rounds for his newly-acquired Glock 17 that he wore holstered cross-draw on his left. Tucked into a waistband holster behind the small of his back was a Sig Sauer P225, a popular single-stack concealed carry weapon that packed a punch. His *just in case* weapon.

Fifty yards behind on his Dyna Street Glide rode Clete Marsden, a pasty-faced Tennessean with a pudding bowl haircut, goatee, and buck teeth, a fellow inmate at the Atlanta Detention Center where Ralph had been awaiting trial for armed robbery.

In Ralph's view, Clete was dumber than a bucketful of rocks. If he was anything to go by, vPox wasn't too picky about who it let live, but as one of only four surviving cons to be released from the facility that morning, he'd allowed Clete to tag along with him. Besides, he owed him an old favor. Ralph was loyal like that.

By the time of his release, he had a pretty good idea of what to expect in the outside world. First, there had been the rumors coming from the fresh meat arriving at the joint. Something about a virus, one even worse than Ebola, raging across the nation.

Then there came vague stuff about it on TV, which he'd watched in the common area of the prison facility. Information was sketchy, and what he heard, he didn't believe. Ralph didn't trust the news anchors on mainstream media. They were simply a bunch of puppets paid to say whatever some rich asshole told them to. Red or blue, it didn't matter. Even an armed robber like Ralph, with only a high school education, and not much of one at that, knew the game was rigged.

Finally, after a few days, another person Ralph didn't trust much either, the president, came on TV and made the announcement that a deadly virus had hit the nation. From where it originated, nobody knew, but it was the most deadly infection known to mankind, and unlike Ebola, it was airborne, which meant it didn't require human contact to be passed on.

The president went on to explain the precautions citizens needed to take so that they didn't become infected. Precautions that, as an inmate at a correctional facility, Ralph knew he wouldn't have a whole lot of control over.

"Damn, sounds like one big clusterfuck," Jim Demerson, his cellmate, had said, slouched on the chair beside him, a worried look on his face.

"How long before it hits here? That's the question on my mind," Ralph replied. "With a bit of luck, it'll hit the COs all at once and we'll just walk right out of the joint."

Demerson chuckled. "Wouldn't that be sweet? Matter of fact, I'd laugh my damn head off."

Turned out, Demerson didn't laugh his head off, though not long after, most of it spilled out through his ears, his mouth, his nose, and his eyes. At the same time, large pustules broke out over his entire body. It wasn't a pretty sight and Ralph did his best to stay away from him. In a six by eight cell, that wasn't nearly far enough. Trouble was, Demerson wasn't going anywhere. The infirmary was full and they weren't taking any more patients.

Thankfully, as far as Ralph was concerned, Demerson croaked two days later. After banging on his cell door for an hour, two correctional officers dressed in HazMat suits came and stuffed Demerson into a body bag while a third stood by the doorway with a Glock leveled at Ralph.

The COs weren't taking any chances. It was the first time Ralph had ever seen a prison guard show up at a cell armed like that. That wasn't standard procedure.

"Hey! What about me?" Ralph yelled as a zipped up Demerson got dragged out of the cell. "Damn it, let me out of this cage! You fuckers ain't even feeding us properly anymore!"

While the whole facility had been in lockdown, Ralph had only been getting one meal a day, shoved in through the bean slot. It was an indication of how bad things were out there.

One of the COs shook his head. "Until the warden says different, you're staying right here, Chambers."

"Yeah? When was the last time he said that to your face?" Ralph asked.

There was no reply.

"He's probably dead already, you dumb fuck!" Ralph screamed as the cell door slammed closed.

For the next while, Ralph checked himself for signs of lesions constantly, certain he was next to become infected. It never happened, though after forty-eight hours with no food served to him, he became convinced he would die from starvation.

Finally, the heavy metal door abruptly swung open. This time, only one CO appeared. He wasn't wearing a HazMat either, though he carried a pistol at his waist. Ralph recognized him right away. It was Johnson. As COs went, he wasn't the worst.

"All right, Chambers, stand up. You're being released."

"Governor's orders?" Ralph asked sarcastically.

"The governor is dead."

Ralph grinned. "Don't say I didn't tell you."

Johnson took him through a series of corridors to one of the facility's interview rooms. Inside were three cons, busily getting dressed into their civilian clothes. One was a black gangbanger, another a guy named Karl Lutz that Ralph didn't care much for. A month ago in the shower room, Lutz tried to bury a five-inch shank in Ralph's back over an earlier dispute. Luckily for Ralph, another con shouted out a warning just in time. That man was Clete Marsden.

"Ralph, you handsome devil!" Clete exclaimed with a goofy grin, giving his scraggly beard a tug. "Damn pox didn't get you neither? What the fuck!"

Ralph ran a hand over the tangle of scars that decorated most of his face. "Looks like I'm pox proof. Goes for you too, you crazy hillbilly." He addressed the CO. "And you, Johnson. You quit wearing the HazMat."

Wordlessly, the CO handed him a plastic bag containing his civilian clothes, then left the room.

Stripping off his prison uniform, Ralph stepped into a pair of old blue jeans, shrugged on his Motorhead T-shirt followed by his biker jacket, then wriggled into a pair of dusty leather boots. Fishing out his wallet, he stuck it in his back pocket, unsure if it would be any use to him anymore. Last, he took out his silver skull ring, kissed its ruby eyes, and stuck it back on his right index finger. Where it belonged.

He stood up from the chair and patted himself down. Six foot four, jet black cropped hair, lean yet bone hard, Ralph "The Face" cut an imposing figure. And he was back in play again.

A few minutes later, Johnson came back. By now, the men were all dressed. He took them out of the room and escorted them down to the release gate.

"How many COs are left?" Ralph asked, strolling alongside Johnson. The boundaries between prisoner and guard had been disappearing every minute since Johnson had let him out of his cell. Four inmates walking through the facility with only the one correctional officer. One who allowed Ralph to walk alongside him.

Johnson hesitated. "There's only two of us. We figured it wasn't fair to keep you guys locked up anymore. Didn't seem any point." Raising a hand up to the CCTV camera, he gave a signal. Ralph heard a loud click and the electronic lock on the release gate opened in front of them.

"What's it like out there?" he asked.

"It's bad. Smells like hell. The dogs are loving it."

"Dangerous?"

Johnson shrugged. "Maybe. Not for someone like you, though." He turned around and pulled the metal door open.

"Still, you can't be too careful, can you?" From behind, Ralph grappled Johnson around the waist and deftly whipped the Glock out of his holster. Pushing him away, Ralph stepped back again.

"What the hell!" Johnson stared in alarm at the pistol now pointed at his chest.

Ralph grinned. "Don't worry, Johnson, you're okay. If it wasn't for you, I'd still be in my cell starving to death." He examined his new toy. "Glock 17? Nice. Built like a friggin' tank, the way a gun ought to be made."

He swiveled the pistol across to Lutz. "As for you, fuckhead...you're definitely *not* okay."

Lutz took a couple of steps back. "Now...now l-look, Chambers," he stuttered, "there's only a few of us lucky enough to survive this damned pox. Come on, cut me a break."

Ralph shook his head. "Can't do that. I'm a man who holds a grudge forever. Besides, you can't expect me to watch my back the whole time I'm out there. I mean, *literally* watch my back." He squeezed the trigger twice and double-tapped Lutz in the chest. With a grunt, the con collapsed onto the floor in a heap.

Giving Johnson a last nod, Ralph stepped out onto Memorial Drive to the stench of garbage and rotting bodies. It didn't bother him. Not one bit. It beat serving a ten year stretch any day of the week.

Ralph was pox proof, and loving it.

CHAPTER 7

Jonah and Colleen walked north up Kirkman Road. They were on their way back to the Sun Ray after spending the past hour in the Publix supermarket. Each wheeled a large trolley in front of them, laden with the provisions they would need for their journey.

Many of the stores they passed had been looted, though most still looked to have plenty of stock left inside. It indicated to Jonah just how few survivors there must be. Earlier, he'd glimpsed a few of them scurrying across the deserted streets. Most appeared to be on their own, a few in pairs. Some wore surgical masks, who Colleen surmised mightn't be immune to the disease but rather had barricaded themselves in their homes to avoid it.

On the way to the supermarket, however, he'd spotted a group of four men that had turned down a side street and disappeared from view. Something about the way they'd strutted down the middle of the road made him wary. Jonah could recognize a skanger a mile away, and he was thankful that, with their backs to him and Colleen, they hadn't spotted the couple. Colleen was right. Tomorrow, their top priority would be to get to a gun shop and arm themselves. In the meantime, in his shopping cart was a baseball bat he'd grabbed from a sports store along the way. A Louisville Slugger, the label said. Sounded good to him.

"Another thing, love," he said, their trolleys rattling noisily down the street. "When we leave town, let's head north. I want to get someplace where I'm not sweating like a pig twenty-four hours a day. Agreed?"

"Agreed," Colleen replied. "There's only so much of this heat I can take too."

"At least you turn brown. I only turn red, then back to white again," Jonah grumbled. "This climate doesn't suit me delicate skin."

Colleen smiled. "We'll leave the day after tomorrow. We should have everything ready by then." She glanced over at him. "When we get back to the hotel, let's find Susan and Klaus, see if they want to come with us too. Is that okay with you?"

Jonah nodded. "All right, though to be honest, I'd be happy to leave Klaus behind. He's a real downer."

Colleen looked at him sharply. "*Jonah*, that's not nice!"

"He's not exactly a barrel of laughs, is he? I had more fun with the undertaker at Uncle Paddy's funeral. What's with the Krauts? They're always so bleedin' serious. I'm mean, did yeh ever watch a German having fun?" Jonah stiffened his shoulders and walked down the street like a robot. "*Ja, vee are having so much fun…Ich bin ein Berliner…haw, haw, haw!*"

Colleen tried to maintain a serious face, but couldn't. "Jonah, that's so mean of you," she said after gaining her composure. "Klaus's wife just died. He's absolutely devastated."

"Ah, true, love," Jonah reflected soberly. "I didn't mean anything bad by it, just having a bit of a laugh. It's not like we couldn't do with a giggle, now is it?"

Above the rattle of their trolleys, behind him, Jonah heard the sound of a can being kicked down the street. He turned his head to see four men following them. They were about fifty yards away and strolled down the middle of the street, shoulders slouched in an exaggerated fashion that exuded menace. He immediately recognized them as the same group he'd seen on their way up to the supermarket earlier.

He thought fast. Ahead was the turn for the Sun Ray, another two hundred yards up the street. There was no way they would make it back to the hotel before the group caught up with them. Anyhow, he didn't want these people to know where they were staying. If they meant trouble, he and Colleen would have to deal with it now.

"Let's take a breather," he said, coming to a stop.

"What? We're almost home. The hotel is just around the corner," Colleen said, pulling up beside him, a frown on her face.

"Exactly." Jonah swiveled his head and indicated back up the street. The men had closed the gap and were now only thirty yards away, marching quickly toward them.

"Oh," Colleen said when she saw them. "What do you think?"

"I think we wait and let them pass."

"What if they don't pass?" she asked nervously.

"Then we deal with it." Jonah mightn't have been the most educated man in the world, but he was good in a tight spot. He'd been getting in and out of scrapes since he was six years old.

Moments later, the group reached them. Without a word, they fanned out around the couple. There was a skinny white guy, two Hispanics and a black dude. Jonah suspected that before the outbreak they hadn't exactly palled together like this. Times had changed.

He eyed them warily. "All right, headerball," he said to the fellow standing in the middle who'd taken another step forward, a squat, well-built Latino with heavily tattooed arms. "What yis looking at? Go on, get on yer way."

The man leered at Jonah. "That's a funny accent you got there. Outrageous I'd call it." He spat on the ground in front of him. "Something tells me you're not from these parts." He turned his head to either side and grinned at his companions like he'd said the funniest thing in the world.

"That's right, Einstein. I thought I'd bring the missus over and show her the apocalypse, drop in and see Donald Duck while we were at it too." If it came to humor, no skanger was ever going to get the better of Jonah Murphy.

One of the other men sniggered. It was the white guy. "Looks like we got a comedian here, and he got a sexy lady with him too." He glanced over at his companion. "What you say, Marco, we take her home with us?"

Jonah plucked the Slugger from out of the trolley and raised it over his shoulder. "Here, enough of that!" he growled. "Go on, scat. Before I bate the head off yeh."

With a grin, Marco reached behind his back and drew out a pistol. "Dude, you're shit out of luck. Looks like you brought a baseball bat to a gunfight."

Jonah's eyes widened, though he continued to keep the bat raised above his head.

"Drop it, or you're a dead man," said the gang leader, aiming his weapon at Jonah's chest.

Jonah wondered whether if he lunged forward, he could smack the guy across the head. He wouldn't survive, but it might give Colleen a chance to make a run for it. A slim chance. Close to zero. Still…it was something.

The white guy stepped in closer to Colleen and made to grab her. Instantly acquiring his new target, Jonah leaned forward and with all his might, swung the bat. He'd crack this bastard's skull open before he died.

Two things happened within a nanosecond of each other. To the sound of a gunshot, the bat made contact with the side of the white guy's head. Staggering back, he collapsed to the ground like a sack of potatoes.

By then, Jonah already knew something was odd. A pistol had fired at point blank range, yet he felt no pain. He turned around to see Marco crouched down on one knee, clutching his side where a trickle of blood dribbled between his fingers.

What the hell was going on?

Another shot sounded, and Jonah realized it was coming from up the street. He looked over to see a gray SUV at the next cross street, sixty yards away. A man leaned out the window holding a rifle.

Crack!

Yet another bullet whined past him.

The two uninjured gang members whipped out their pistols, firing back at the vehicle.

Jonah needed no further prompting. Dropping the Slugger, he seized Colleen's arm. "Come on!" he yelled.

The two raced down the street in the opposite direction to the SUV as the gunfire intensified. Any second, Jonah expected a stray bullet to hit one of them. Reaching the corner of the block, he glanced back to see the SUV swerve away from the curb and roar off.

"Keep going!" he yelled at Colleen. "Leg it!"

The two continued to run at full pelt. A hundred yards farther, they reached a narrow side street. Jonah ushered Colleen around the corner and out of sight, and the two came to a halt. Leaning over, hands on their knees, they caught their breaths.

"Jonah…" Colleen gasped between breaths. "Who the hell was that?"

"Haven't a breeze," Jonah replied, his lungs heaving. "Guess not everyone out there is a complete skanger. That geezer just saved our lives."

He peeked around the corner. There was no one on the street. "We'll give it another few minutes, then I'll sneak back up there, see what's going on."

"Jonah, are you crazy?" Colleen cried out in alarm. "What you want to do that for?"

"We still got our shopping back there. Maybe the skangers left it behind. I don't want to be fetching all that stuff again. Do you?"

Three minutes later, leaving Colleen out of sight, Jonah stealthily headed back up to the corner of the block.

Peering cautiously around, he saw that only one gang member remained. It was Marco. He sat on the ground, leaning up against the wall. There was no sign of his pistol. Behind him, standing where they'd left them, were the two supermarket trolleys.

Jonah stepped around the corner. "Yo, gobshite!" he called out.

Marco jerked his head toward him, a look of surprise on his face. The lower portion of his T-shirt and his jeans were soaked in blood. It had spilled onto the sidewalk too.

"What the fuck you doing here?" he said, his voice weak.

Jonah pointed over at the two trolleys.

The Latino shook his head. "Crazy mofo."

"You still got that pistol?"

"No, man. They took it off me and left me here to die."

Jonah walked cautiously over and stared down at the Latino. "Sorry to hear that, bud. But see, this here is the apocalypse. It's not easy making *real* friends." He looked around for his bat. Spotting it by the far side of the trolleys, he strolled over and picked it up.

"Hey, what you doing?" Marco asked warily as Jonah walked back over to him.

Jonah raised the bat high in the air. "I'm putting you out of your misery, headerball, that's what."

Swinging the bat, he smashed it across the side of Marco's head. Soundlessly, he toppled over and slumped onto the sidewalk.

Jonah chucked the Slugger into one of the trolleys, then grasped both of them, one in each hand, and began hauling them back toward where he'd left Colleen. That was one dead skanger the world was better off without. He was sure it wouldn't be the last one he'd run into.

CHAPTER 8

At 4:05 p.m. Cody left the house. This time he drove Joe's car, an old Chevy Malibu. It was a real beater, but still had a half tank of gas in it. It had been a busy day and he was running late. He had plenty of news for Walter and Pete, and was excited to tell them about it.

He drove south on Interstate 75 and took the I-640 loop heading east, then swung around the back of the city. Twenty minutes later, he reached Magnolia Avenue.

Approaching the gas station, he immediately saw something was up. Several vehicles sat parked across all three entrances, blocking them. He drove slowly by and spotted Walter. He stood in the middle of the forecourt, a group of men standing around him. They carried rifles and wore pistols by their waists.

One of the men was huge, about six foot six, with massive shoulders, and completely bald apart from some long, straggly hair at the back. Standing beside him was a young woman who in comparison looked tiny. She had short bottle-blonde hair, and wore a tight-fitting white T-shirt, cutoff jeans, and high heels.

Walter stared at Cody grimly as he passed by. He made no attempt to show he recognized him. Cody took that as a warning.

At that moment, one of the men turned around. Leering, he waved him on. Cody didn't need any further encouragement. Jamming his foot on the pedal, he picked up speed and continued down Magnolia in the direction of the city.

In a state of shock, he drove several blocks until the Chevron station was out of sight, then took a right onto Cherry Street and pulled up at the curb. He cut the engine and took a deep breath. Looking around, he remembered that Walter lived on one of the streets nearby, though he could no longer remember its name. That wasn't the reason he'd stopped here though. He stopped because he needed to think.

In the days and months to come, fuel would become an increasingly valuable resource. With no police or army to maintain order, it appeared that one of the newly-formed gangs Walter had warned about the other night had commandeered the gas station. In this new world, everyone found themselves in, possession had quickly become ten/tenths of the law.

Reluctantly, Cody decided it would be best to head home. Returning to the station would not only be dangerous for him, but might endanger Walter too. Left undisturbed, hopefully the gang wouldn't harm him. His mind made up, he started the engine and drove north up Cherry, where at the top of the street he could pick up the westbound entrance to I-40.

A few blocks up, he reached Woodbine Avenue. Without making a conscious decision, he swung onto it and headed east. Woodbine ran all the way to the Knoxville Zoo. It also led to the back of the Chevron station. No matter what the logical part of his mind told him, leaving Walter to the whims of a street gang just didn't sit right with Cody.

When he reached Castle Street, the road that ran along the east side of the station, he turned right and headed down toward Magnolia. Soon the red sign of the AutoZone across the street from the Chevron loomed in front of him.

Cutting the Chevy's engine, he coasted another fifty yards before turning into the parking lot of a small two-story apartment block.

He reached over and grabbed his newly-acquired Ruger SR-556 carbine from off the passenger seat. Earlier that day, following Walter's instructions, he'd picked it up at the Guardian Armory at the Seven Oaks Mall fifteen miles west of Knoxville. Behind the counter, he'd found the 5.56 NATO rounds for it, just where Walter described they would be. After a little more searching, he found plenty of .45 ACP ammunition for the Kimber 1911 too.

He got out of the Malibu, slung the Ruger over his shoulder, and headed toward Magnolia Avenue, sticking to the shadows as much as possible. Two minutes later, he reached a small lane that ran parallel to the back of the gas station. Crossing it, he darted down the grass verge that led to a paved yard at the rear of the building.

He inched along the back wall and stuck his head around the corner to see a dark sedan parked at the top, whose nose peeked out onto the forecourt. In a low crouch, he crept to it, then scuttled around the side and peered over the sedan's hood.

Fifty feet away, Walter knelt on the ground, at the spot where he'd pointed out the underground storage tanks the previous night. He was in the process of fixing a length of hose to what Cody presumed was a pump of some description.

Two men stood over him. Other than a menacing presence, they didn't seem to have harmed him. The gang must have driven by earlier while Walter was rigging up the system. With a bit of luck, they would let him go once they'd fueled up.

Standing nearby, the big man and the girl watched the proceedings. Next to them was a skinny guy. He looked familiar. With a start, Cody saw it was Pete. Inwardly, he groaned. This must be the gang Pete had been thinking of joining. He must have told them of Walter's plans to rig a pump for the underground tanks. Rage went through Cody. Pete had betrayed Walter. His price of entry into the gang.

The big guy was talking, speaking in a gruff low-toned voice. "Pete tells me you're real smart, Walter. Said you were an engineer in the military. That where they taught you shit like this?"

Walter chuckled. "Don't know about being smart, but it's where I learned this shit all right. Though in practice, most of the time I just blew things up." Although his tone was friendly, Cody could detect an undercurrent of tension in it.

"Maybe you ought to consider joining my group. I could do with someone with your skills."

Walter shook his head. "Thanks for the offer, Mason, but see, I don't plan on staying in the city much longer. I'll be gone in a couple of days." He stood up and rubbed the dirt off his hands. "We're done. The system is set up. Why don't somebody go fetch the gas cans and I'll start filling them up."

Mason pointed over to one of the pickups and ordered the two men standing next to Walter to go fetch the cans. "So where you planning on going?" he asked Walter while they waited for the men to come back.

"I guess I'll hit the hills somewhere nearby. Plenty of forest and rivers where a man can live off the land. With my wife and daughter dead, I could do with some time on my own."

The two crew members returned, each carrying several large gas cans. Walter took one. Kneeling down again, he screwed the cap off and stuck the end of the hose into it. There was the sound of a small motor running, then before long, liquid gushed into the container.

"It's working," Walter said with satisfaction.

"Of course…to hunt in the forest, you need to stay pretty mobile, don't you? It's not like they keep the deer in pens there, do they?"

Cody watched in horror as Mason withdraw his pistol from his waist holster. He strode toward Walter, who had his back to him, aimed at his left leg, and fired.

The gunshot rang out harshly around the forecourt, followed by a loud yell. Dropping the pump, Walter lay on the ground clutching his lower leg. "What the hell you do that for?" he cried out.

"Your vacation's been canceled," Mason informed him, casually slotting his pistol back in its holster. Don't worry, we'll get that patched up for you. Meantime, best you stick with us. The city's getting dangerous. Who knows, in the coming days you might decide it's not such a bad idea to join me after all."

"Sonofabitch!" Walter gasped under his breath.

Mason stared at the two men standing beside Walter. "Come on. You've seen how the pump works. Start filling those cans." He headed across the forecourt to where a black GMC Canyon stood parked.

With a look of dismay, Pete rushed over to Walter and crouched down beside him. "You okay?" he asked.

Walter pushed him away. "Get away from me," he said angrily.

"I'm sorry. I-I never meant this to turn out this way." Pete grasped Walter under his arms and dragged him to his feet.

Transfixed by the sudden turn of events, Cody decided that now was the time to act. Gritting his teeth, he unslung the Ruger, switched the selector to its firing position, and leapt up from behind the sedan's hood. He brought the rifle up to his shoulder and fired off several shots in the air.

Walter and Pete stared over at him, a look of shock on their faces.

"It's me—Cody!" he shouted. "Get over here!"

Glancing at each other, the two began running toward him, Walter hobbling badly, using Pete for support.

Meanwhile, Mason, who'd reached the far end of the forecourt, pulled out his pistol and fired in their direction.

The two men who'd crouched down by the pump grabbed their rifles and stood up too.

Before they could take aim, Cody swiveled the Ruger at them. Aiming it at the quicker of the two, he pulled the trigger.

Two shots. *Pop! Pop!*

With a grunt, the man dropped to his knees. His rifle fell out of his hands and clattered to the ground in front of him.

Cody aimed at the second man, who by now had his rifle up to his shoulder. Another two shots, and he staggered. Clutching his rifle, he keeled over and fell to the ground.

Walter and Pete reached Cody and ducked around the back of the sedan. The gang, which had scattered around the forecourt, were firing wildly now, and the three took cover around the corner of the building. The thin metal of a sedan wasn't going to offer them much in the way of protection from heavy gunfire.

"Good work, kid. Where's your car?" Walter gasped. There was a thick film of sweat on his face from the pain.

"Too far for you to run," Cody told him. He peeked around the corner and saw there was no one in sight. His fear now was that Mason would send some of his crew around the far side of the station and block their escape route.

He thought fast. Pulling out the keys to Joe's car, he handed them to Pete, then pointed behind him. "Go fetch the car. It's parked in front of the apartment block at the back of the station. A green Chevy Malibu, beat to hell. You can't miss it."

There was a look in Pete's eye that told Cody he was anxious to redeem himself. Given the trouble he'd gotten them into, he still had plenty of work to do.

Snatching the keys, Pete ran along the sidewall of the station. Cody breathed a sigh of relief after he'd sprinted up the grass verge and crossed the lane without being shot at.

Cody pulled the Kimber from out of his jacket and handed it to Walter.

"All right kid," Walter said, taking the weapon. "You watch the front of the station, I'll go down the end and stop anyone coming around the back."

Though injured, Walter's voice was calm and authoritative. Despite their precarious situation, Cody felt his jangled nerves soothe a little. Walter limped along the side wall in the direction Pete had gone. He stopped at the corner and peered around the back of the station. He didn't fire the Kimber, which Cody took as a good sign.

Out front, he heard the sound of an engine starting. When the gang had scattered, two had run toward a blue Nissan Patrol, parked across one of the entranceways. Sure enough, a moment later, the Patrol pulled away, facing downtown. As soon as it took off, however, it made a U-turn and headed back in Pete's direction.

Cody took that as his cue to open fire. He flipped up the Ruger's rear sight and lined up his shot through the peephole. As the Nissan straightened out on the road, he aimed through the driver's window, releasing several shots. A moment later, the pickup veered off the road, bumped over the curb, and ran across the AutoZone parking lot before finally coming to a stop. Cody kept his eye on it. No one made an attempt to get out. If anyone was still alive inside, they were keeping their heads low.

Behind him, he heard the sound of gunshots. Glancing back, he saw Walter leaning around the far corner, firing the Kimber in single spaced shots. A volley of gunfire opened up in reply.

At that moment, the Malibu came charging down the lane, its engine screaming. Veering sharply, it swooped down the grass verge and careened across the yard, skidding to a stop alongside Walter, who yanked open the back door and clambered inside. Then the Malibu raced along the side of the station and jerked to a stop several feet from Cody. Running across to it, he opened the door and jumped in beside Walter.

"Floor it!" he shouted.

With a jerk, the car shot across the forecourt and out onto the main road. Cody buzzed down the window and poked the Ruger out while, behind them, several of the gang members started shooting. Cody unleashed the Ruger and they quickly ducked for cover again.

Pete straightened out the wheel and tore down Magnolia. After a few blocks, Walter ordered him to slow down and directed him down a side street.

For the next few minutes, the Malibu weaved through the back streets until they passed a series of interconnected, one-story buildings that took up an entire block. A sign outside read Austin East High School. Driving around the back, they drew up alongside the curb.

"Are we safe here?" Pete asked anxiously, cutting the engine. "I don't think we're going to outrun anyone in this heap."

"We're good. No one followed us," Walter told him.

Pete breathed a sigh of relief.

"How's your wound?" Cody asked.

Up till now, Walter hadn't got a chance to examine it. He leaned against the passenger door and carefully raised his leg up onto the seat. Staring down at it, Cody saw a dark stain in the middle of his left calf.

"There's the entry wound," Walter said, studying it carefully. He peered around the other side. "And here's where it exited. I got lucky. It didn't hit bone, and no artery's been hit." He winced. "Hurts like a bitch, though."

"Thank God for that," Cody said gratefully.

"Main risk is infection," Walter continued. "I need to get disinfectant and surgical gauze. Antibiotics too. I got isopropyl and bandages at home. Trouble is, we might run into Mason and his crew if we head back that way. Best if we pick it up somewhere else."

"The Physicians Regional Medical Center is close to here," Cody said, thinking about the first hospital he'd taken Joe to the other day. "How about we go there?"

Walter nodded. "That'll do. All right, start her up, Pete. I'll direct you."

"Hold on, one minute," Cody said. He reached out his hand and indicated to Walter that he return the Kimber.

Walter smiled. "Sure, kid. Wasn't planning on stealing it. By the way, nice shooting back there. Your father taught you good."

Without a word, Cody took the pistol from him. Leaning forward between the front seats, he jammed the muzzle into the side of Pete's head. "All right," he said through clenched teeth. "Before we go anywhere, you got some explaining to do."

CHAPTER 9

Located on Courtland Street, the Atlanta Hilton was in the heart of the convention district and took up an entire city block. It was an impressive-looking building, lots of glass and steel, and had a sky bridge that connected it to the neighboring Marriott on the far side of the street. Ralph was torn choosing between the two. Finally, he settled on the Hilton. More for the name than anything else.

"Color me impressed," he said as he and Clete dismounted their machines outside the huge Y-shaped building and stared up at the shiny three-story atrium that served as the main entranceway to the hotel. "We should stay a couple of nights and chill the hell out. S'okay, this one's on me, I'll take care of the bill.

Clete grinned. "Gee, thanks. When we get to our rooms, let's order champagne. I'll arrange with the bellhop to bring a couple of girls over. They'll do that if you tip them right, you know."

Ralph gave him a look. "That what you did last time you were here, hot shot?"

The two entered the building through a set of automatic doors that someone had already busted open. Strolling across the intricately-laid stone floor, they wandered into the spacious lobby, Ralph with his Bushmaster in hand,

Clete with his Colt M4 carbine. As expected, it was totally deserted. No one at reception or at the bell stand.

Over on the left, Ralph spotted the bar. He nudged Clete. "Don't know about you, but I could murder a drink. Come on."

The two headed inside to the counter. "Fix me a Jack Daniels and Coke," Ralph ordered. "I'll be at my usual spot." He sauntered over to one of the tables nearby and plonked himself down in a comfortable chair, resting his rifle against the side.

He looked around his surroundings. "Man, this beats a six by eight cell any day of the week," he said with a satisfied sigh. "Yo, bring me over a plate of crackers!" he yelled at Clete. "I'm getting peckish again."

A few hours ago, the two had broken into a high-end grocery store and gorged themselves on smoked ham, cheese, olives, and other delicacies. Not having eaten in so long, Ralph was getting hungry again.

It was dark inside the lounge without any power. As Ralph's eyes got used to the gloom, he spotted a blur of movement over at the far side of the room.

He leaped out of his seat and whipped the Glock from out of his holster. "Clete!" he hissed. A moment later, Clete poked his head around the counter, a questioning look on his face. Waving his pistol, Ralph motioned toward the far side of the room.

He made his way cautiously over, relaxing when he got closer. A woman with wavy salon-styled brunette hair sat alone at a table, her feet tucked up in front of her on the armchair like a cat.

She wore a tight-fitting cream sweater, a black leotard, and heels, straightening up as he approached, to reveal a shapely set of muscular legs.

Dancer's legs, Ralph thought to himself. On the table beside her was a tumbler of whiskey, a bottle of Laphroaig next to it.

She stared at Ralph, unfazed by his presence. That included the nine millimeter pistol he pointed at her chest.

"Well howdy," she murmured. "Seeing as that's a gun in your hand, I guess you're not pleased to see me, huh?"

"What the hell are you doing here?" Ralph growled. He looked around the room suspiciously, as if he was missing something. Like the girl was bait, and a heavily-armed SWAT team was about to storm the bar at any moment.

Closer to her, he saw just how beautiful she was. She had Asian-shaped green eyes, light-brown skin, and a delicate oval face with perfect bone structure. She looked straight off the cover of a magazine.

"Isn't a girl entitled to have a quiet drink on her own while she contemplates her woes?" She patted the chair next to her invitingly. "How about you sit down and I'll tell you all about them."

Ralph hesitated a moment, then holstered his weapon and sat down beside her. "We all got woes, lady," he said gruffly, unable to take his eyes off her. "How about you start by telling me your name?"

"Maya. And you?"

"Ralph." He waved a hand at Clete, who had stopped ten feet away and stood watching the two uncertainly, his M4 still up at his shoulder. "What's keeping you? Bring my drink over." He shook his head as Clete lowered his rifle and headed back to the bar. "Hard to find good help these days."

Maya chuckled. "Friend of yours, I take it?"

"I guess. I'm kind of short on friends right now."

"Aren't we all? Last time I logged onto Facebook, they told me I had more friends than I think. I'm not so sure though. I think they might be lying."

Ralph chuckled. "That's funny."

Maya stared at him closely. "No offense, but what's with the face?"

Ralph ran his hand over the mess of scars on his face, the result of several knife fights over the years. "You're not the first to ask. Let's just say I ran into a little trouble once. Come to think of it, more than once."

"Looks like you run into it pretty hard. Lucky for you, I got a thing about ugly men."

Ralph grinned. "Must be my lucky day. This morning I was locked up in a cell, starving to death. Six hours later, I'm in the Hilton with a beautiful girl who likes ugly men."

"Only because the good-looking ones are all dead. Sorry, did I forget to mention that part?"

The grin on Ralph's face widened. He liked this girl already. Maya cruised right at his speed, with her foot mashed to the floor. "So what's going on?" he asked. "You get here before the shit went down, or did you book in on the special like me?"

"I got here two days before everything went to hell. Out of the blue, a friend of mine came to town and invited me over." Maya shrugged. "Seeing as I wasn't doing anything at the time, I mosied right over."

Ralph stared at her carefully, sizing up what she just told him. "Nice to have friends like that. I take it he's dead? That's what the odds say anyway."

Maya nodded. "I left him in his room and took another one across the hall. Sad, but there you go. Sometimes in life you got to move on."

At that moment, Clete came over with their drinks. Placing them down, he dragged another chair over from the next table and sat down beside them.

"Clete, Maya. Maya, Clete," Ralph said by way of introduction. "Biggest goofball I know. And that's before the whole damned world went and died on me."

"Hey!" Clete protested. "That's not a nice way to introduce somebody." He flashed Maya a toothy grin. "Don't worry, I'm a darn sight smarter than Ralph makes out."

Maya smiled back at him sweetly. "That's a relief to know. Tell me, how long are you two planning on staying here?" she asked, looking from one man to the other.

"Don't know, we just got here," Ralph replied. "I'm liking it already."

"Sure, but we can't stay here forever. You know that, don't you?"

"Why the hell not?"

"Food and water will run out soon. There may not be many survivors, but they're all stocking up with as much as they can and leaving the city. Gangs are starting to form too. I see them on the streets as I drive by. They're not walking around with happy smiley faces either."

Ralph shrugged. "There'll be gangs everywhere, not just the cities. You're right about the food and water, though. Clete, we should stock up on stuff tomorrow, before it all goes."

Maya took a sip from her drink. "Maybe I could tag along with you guys and get my supplies at the same time. It's not easy being a woman on her own in times like these."

Ralph had no problem with that. He could stare at that face all day long. "That's fine with me. How about you, Clete?"

"Fine with me too. It's dangerous out there for a good-looking woman like yourself." Clete chuckled. "Don't worry, you'll be safe with us. Lucky for you, me and Ralph are kinda dangerous too."

Maya smiled. "You have no idea how happy that makes me." She raised her glass at the two. "Let's toast to the start of a beautiful friendship."

Ralph lifted his glass. "I'll drink to that...all night long."

CHAPTER 10

Leaning on Pete's shoulder, Walter hobbled across the hospital parking lot behind Cody, who led the way to the ER center. Unlike the last occasion he was here, there were no National Guard soldiers blocking their way. It was now dusk, and inside the building was eerily deserted. Cody panned his keyring flashlight around the waiting room, the smell of disinfectant strong in his nostrils.

"All clear," he whispered, beckoning Pete and Walter to follow him down the aisle where, at the end, a set of double doors led into the treatment rooms.

By now, Cody's anger with Pete had subsided. He wasn't a bad person, he just made a terrible mistake introducing Mason to Walter in order to join his gang. He'd no idea just how violent and unscrupulous Mason would be.

"So stupid of me," he'd said in the car earlier, shaking his head forlornly. "Guess I was too scared to leave the city with you guys, and too scared to stay on by myself."

"You got no choice but to come with us now. You still owe me, buddy," Walter had said with a chuckle.

Amazed by Walter's equanimity and the lack of ill will he felt toward the man who'd nearly gotten him killed, Cody had no choice but to act likewise. Luckily for both of them, Pete had gone on to quickly make amends. Without his help,

Cody doubted he and Walter would have gotten out of the gas station alive.

When he was about to push open the door to the treatment rooms, something in the corner of the room caught Cody's eye. He shone his flashlight over to witness a gruesome sight. A pile of bodies lay stacked up on top of each other, their faces racked in an assortment of hideous grimaces. Too sick to take the bodies to the morgue, the ER personnel had disposed of them here, Cody guessed.

"Jesus," Pete muttered. "It's like a scene out of *The Walking Dead*."

Walter hobbled forward. "Come on," he said grimly. "Let's get what we need and get out of here."

They passed through the double doors and walked down a long corridor with ER rooms to either side. Cody pushed open the door to one on his left. Inside, a nurse in blue scrubs lay on a gurney, her face directed toward the ceiling. Beside her, a doctor wearing white gloves sat slumped in a chair, a stethoscope dangling off his chest. Both had the same ravaged faces that Cody had seen on Joe and Chrissie the other day. Stepping slowly back, he exited the room and closed the door behind him.

They checked the rest of the treatment rooms. All contained one or more dead bodies. Standing by the door to the last one at the top of the hall, Walter pointed into the room. "All right, kid, see that crash cart in the corner? Bring it out here."

Cody went in and wheeled out a blue and white plastic trolley. While he aimed his flashlight at it, Walter rummaged through the drawers, pulling out various items. "Scissors…gauze…tape…sterile   pads…bandages…better take some sutures and needles too. Once I've drained the wound, I might need to stitch it." He straightened up. "All right, that'll do. I can pick up antibiotics at a pharmacy tomorrow. Let's go."

The three headed back down the corridor again, through the waiting room, and into the parking lot.

"Where we going to patch you up?" Cody asked, taking the keys to the Malibu from Pete and opening the driver's door. "You can both come back to my place if you want."

"Might be the best thing," Walter said, after thinking about it. "Mason and his gang hang out on the east side. That's too close to where me and Pete live."

Cody started the engine and pulled out of the lot. Avoiding the freeway, he drove through North Knoxville until he caught the Central Avenue Pike. A short time later, they passed by the Starbucks and Hooters, where Cody turned west onto Merchant Drive and went under the I-75 underpass, heading toward West Inskip Drive.

"By the way, with all that's happened, I didn't get a chance to tell you my news," he said, pulling into his driveway and killing the engine.

"What's that?" Walter and Pete asked in unison.

Cody grinned. "I made some new friends today. While I was out shopping, I bumped into another group of survivors. There's eight of them."

Walter stared at him sharply. "What kind of group?" he asked warily. "I didn't particularly care for the one we met today."

"They're not a gang," Cody assured him. "As far as I can tell, they're good people. They're leaving the city tomorrow too." He hesitated. "Maybe we should go meet them. If we all get along, we could drive out together. Like in a convoy. Safer that way."

"Who's in charge of this group?" Walter asked. "They got a leader?"

"Yeah. A guy named Chris. He was some corporate bigwig before everything went down. He's nothing like Mason," Cody added emphatically. "He's got principles. He's looking to set up a community in the wilderness somewhere. They're real serious about this. They've already got themselves Winnebagos and travel trailers. Maybe we should think about doing something like that too." He looked at them both. "What do you guys think?"

"A trailer's a great idea!" Pete exclaimed. "A whole lot better than living in a damned tent. How about it, Walter? We go check them out tomorrow?"

"All right, no harm in doing that," Walter said slowly. "But Cody, let's not be too hasty. We'll just tag along for the moment. A group provides greater safety, but like I told you, you lose a lot of your freedom for that."

"Cool!" Cody said excitedly. "First thing tomorrow, let's go get pickups and trailers. If you two both get along with Chris, we'll head out of town with his group. Either way, it's about time we found ourselves some new homes!"

CHAPTER 11

Turned out that before the pandemic, Maya worked at the Cheetah Lounge, a high class strip joint on Spring Street, a few blocks north of the Hilton. A wealthy businessman had taken a real shine to her, "totally besotted", according to Maya. He'd wined and dined her, then subsequently installed her in his room the whole time he was in Atlanta closing some bigshot deal. He'd bought her nice clothes, took her out to fancy restaurants, even bought her flowers one evening – which Maya had appreciated, especially the diamond necklace he'd popped inside the accompanying envelope.

"No doubt about it, George was a sweet guy. Tons of charisma," Maya said, wrapping up her story. Ralph detected a tinge of sadness in her voice. It didn't make him jealous. George was dead, and Ralph could get her a diamond necklace any day of the week. He wasn't so sure about the flowers, though.

"I saw a movie like that once," he said as the two lay naked in bed, in the biggest room they could find on the third floor of the hotel, a bottle of Laphroig on her bedstand, Jack Daniels and a pack of Marlboros on Ralph's. Also on his side was his backup pistol, his Sig P225.

Just in case.

"It was called *Pretty Woman*. Starred Richard Gere and Julia Roberts." He stubbed his cigarette out in the ashtray. "Kind of a sweet movie, to be honest."

Maya stared at him. "Julia Roberts played a hooker in that movie, I stripped for a living. Big difference." She let out a throaty chuckle. "Anyhow, I never would have taken someone like you to have a soft spot for rom coms. Did you cry at the end? The truth now."

Ralph grinned. "I might have choked up a little. Bank robbers got hearts too, you know." He glanced over at her. ""If it wasn't for vPox, would you and George have ridden off into the sunset, just like Richard and Julia?"

"No, George was married," Maya answered. "Childhood sweetheart, no prenup. She would have taken him to the cleaners. Nope, it was never going anywhere." She ran her fingers through the thick black hairs on his chest. "Me and you though, now that might have legs."

Ralph reached a hand out lazily for another cigarette. The two had gotten pretty comfortable with one another. In this crazy new world, three hours was a long time.

"Like you say, all the good-looking men are dead. A guy like me's got to fancy his chances."

Maya smiled. "Behind those scars, you're not so bad looking. How exactly did you get them?"

Ralph shrugged. "I'm forty-three-years old. Spent fifteen of them in the joint. Shit happens when you do time."

"That's one thing you never need to worry about again. Doing time."

"Damn straight. I could be dead by tomorrow, but it won't be in a cage. This is a one-day-at-a-time world we're living in now."

Maya shook her head. "No it's not, Ralph. I was serious about what I said earlier. We need to start planning. We got to get out of the city, and soon."

"Yeah? And go where exactly?"

"Somewhere there's food and water. And I don't mean out of a bottle, or off a shelf. I'm talking about a river for drinking water, a forest for hunting. Like it or not, that's what's coming next."

Ralph looked doubtful. "I hate the damned countryside. Lived in cities my entire life. Don't know nothing about hunting either."

Maya looked at him quizzically. "How come? Seeing as you're a bank robber and all?"

"They're two different things, that's why. Bank robbers live in cities, 'cos that's where the banks are. Hillbillies live in the boonies, 'cos that's where the squirrels are."

Maya laughed. "You're only forty-three. You'll learn soon enough how to hunt."

Ralph mulled this over. "Now, Clete, he's from Tennessee. A certified genuine hillbilly. Grew up hunting, fishing, and trapping. In the can he never shut up about it."

"Where in Tennessee?"

"Can't remember exactly. Somewhere near the Blue Ridge Mountains if I remember right."

"Maybe we should gather supplies and head there," Maya mused. "I'm sure Clete will be more than happy to get back to his old stomping grounds. What do you say?"

Ralph looked at her suspiciously. "Will I have to chew 'baccy and wear flannel shirts and dungarees?"

"That's up to you. If you go down that route, you'll need a mullet haircut to go with it. Personally, I prefer your biker look."

Ralph patted the bed. "Wherever we go, let's get a bed just like this." He grinned. "They're a lot of fun."

"Unfortunately, we'll need to be practical. Get something that actually fits in a trailer."

Ralph stared at her in alarm. "A *trailer*? You really are talking hillbilly shit, aren't you?"

"That's right, baby, I am." With one deft move, Maya rolled over on top of Ralph's waist. Straddling her long legs to either side of him, she leaned over. "In the meantime, let's make the most of our big comfortable bed, shall we?"

CHAPTER 12

Early the following morning, Jonah left the hotel, leaving Colleen behind with strict instructions not to even as much as poke her nose out the door until he returned. Having grown up in the flats, Jonah didn't scare easily. However, his encounter with the skangers the previous day had shaken him. He shuddered to think what might have happened to Colleen had the passing stranger not helped them out. He vowed never to let himself get caught out like that again. Today, he intended to tool up. Big time.

Jumping into his Taurus rental, he headed out of the tiny parking lot at the back of the Sun Ray in search of a gun store. With the Internet down, in a city he barely knew, that might prove difficult. Hopefully, he would come across a sign in a window somewhere that said: GUNS. That would make things easier.

Jonah had never handled a pistol before. People didn't own them in Ireland. Not legally, anyway. Only bank robbers and drug lords had them. He'd come across a fellow showing one off in the flats once. Jonah had refused to handle it. Only a gobshite would risk leaving his dabs on a shooter.

He drove north up Kirkman Road in the direction of the Pines Shopping Center. He and Colleen had visited it when they'd first arrived in the city. To either side of him, the streets were deserted. People had either left town or were keeping a low profile. It was too dangerous out there to be lollygagging about the place, that was for sure.

Passing Eagle Nest Park on his right, he spotted a tall, gangling figure fifty yards ahead. With short, dark hair thinning on top, the man wore a striped-blue polo shirt, khaki shorts, and sandals. As he got closer, Jonah recognized him. It was Klaus, from Room 22 at the Sun Ray.

Jonah buzzed down the front passenger window and drew up alongside him. "Yo, Klaus!" he called, leaning across.

The startled German stopped in his tracks. Stooping over, he stared in through the window. "Jonah!" he said in his heavily-accented English. "You gave me a terrible fright."

"Sorry bud, but you shouldn't be walking around here on your own, it's too dangerous. There's mangy-looking skangers all over the place. Me and Colleen ran into some yesterday."

"My car is out of petrol. Without power, I can't fill it up." Klaus pointed up the road. "I need to get to the shopping center and get supplies."

Jonah patted the seat beside him. "Just so happens I'm passing that way. Hop in. I'll give you a lift."

Klaus gratefully pulled open the door and got into the car. "Thank you," he said, sitting down and immediately putting on his safety belt.

Jonah chuckled. "Ah now, there's no need for that. It's not like someone's going to give us a ticket. Though with my driving, maybe yer better off leaving it on."

"Yes, just a habit," Klaus replied stiffly, making no effort to remove the belt.

As they drove on, a thought occurred to Jonah. "Yer not packing a shooter by any chance, are yeh?"

Klaus stared at him blankly. "A shooter?"

"A gun…a pistol. Have you got yourself one yet?"

Klaus shook his head. "Why, are you looking for one?"

"Sure am, bud. The streets are getting meaner every day. We need to protect ourselves. Yeh fancy coming with me and finding a gun shop?"

"I don't know. I…I've never fired a gun before," Klaus said hesitantly.

"You, me, and the Pope, bro, but if there was ever a time to learn, this'd be it."

They reached the top of Kirkman and were approaching the shopping center on their left. Jonah looked over at Klaus questioningly.

"I think you're right," the German said. "There's no longer the police to protect us. We can't rely on anyone but ourselves."

"Good man," Jonah said, delighted to have some company. Even if it might be with quite literally the dullest man on the planet. "Right, keep yer eyes peeled and let's see if we can find one of these gun store jobbies. Watch out for the skangers while yer at it. No telling what they might be up to."

The two men cruised the streets looking out for a gun store. "Jonah? That's a funny name," Klaus said after a while. "I don't think I've ever met one before."

Jonah chuckled. "I got given that name when I was in the merchant navy. I used to get into all sorts of trouble, always dragging me friends into it too. After we'd been hauled in front of the captain for the umpteenth time and given a right rollicking, they told me, 'Brendan, we're keeping away from you, yer a right bleedin' Jonah.' The name kinda stuck after that."

He stared over at the blank expression on Klaus's face.

"Sorry," the German said apologetically. "But you talk so fast, and your accent…it's very strong."

Jonah grinned. "Yer a fine one to be talking about accents. Tell yeh what? Say *Vorsprung durch technik mein liebchen, drei times* and we'll call it quits." He craned his neck forward. "Wait a mo…what do have we here?"

The two were downtown now, in an area called South Division. A few hundred yards away, two men walked down the street. Though they had their backs to him, Jonah could make out that each held a rifle in their hands, the muzzles pointing toward the ground.

Getting closer, he saw both were muscular, with close-cropped hair. They wore camo pants and tight fitting T-shirts, and walked with a certain gait. Jonah took them for military men.

"How about we have a word with these lads? They don't look like skangers," he said slowing down. "Maybe they can help us."

Klaus looked at him in consternation. "Jonah, they've got guns."

"And what are we looking for right now? Don't worry, I'll give them a quick toot of the horn first so we don't scare them."

With the edge of his palm, Jonah gave the horn a slap. The switch on the steering wheel must have been stiff, however, because the horn didn't sound. Pressing on it harder, it suddenly blared out a long, loud blast.

"*Jaypers!*" Jonah cried out in alarm.

In front of them, the two men swiveled around. Spreading out, both raised their rifles to their shoulders and pointed them at the Taurus.

"*Ach, mein Gott!*" Klaus screamed hysterically. "They're going to kill us!"

Jonah slammed his foot on the brakes and threw his arm out the window, waving it manically at the two men. "Lads, lads, yer all right!" he yelled. "We're only looking for directions!"

The two men looked at each other, then cautiously approached the car from either side. A moment later, Jonah stared down the barrel of a rifle.

"Mister, that wasn't a smart thing to do," growled a man with bulging biceps and three days' worth of growth on his face. "You looking to get yourself killed?"

"Sorry, didn't mean that," Jonah said sheepishly. "I was only looking to give yis a quick beep. Something's wrong with the bleedin' horn, so there is."

The man chuckled. "Say, is that an Irish accent?" he asked, lowering his rifle.

Jonah nodded.

The man broke out into a big smile. "Well how about that? My great great granddaddy was from Skibereen, County Cork. You ever hear of the place?" He squatted beside the window, staring in at Jonah.

"Been there many a time. For the fishing mainly," Jonah replied. He'd been in similar conversations like this before. The Yanks loved a natter about the old sod. This was the first one since the end of the world though. It felt a little surreal.

The man scratched his chin. "Well, I'll be damned. I take it you were on vacation when vPox went down?"

"Yeah, I was taking the missus on holliers," Jonah replied. "I tell yeh, it's been bleedin' brutal."

The man frowned. "*Holliers?* What the hell's that?"

"Eh, a holiday, bud. You know, Waterworld, Disney, that sort of thing."

"A vacation? Got you. I'm sure sorry you got caught up in all this. Not what you were expecting when you got here, right?"

Jonah stared at the man. That was putting it mildly. At that moment, his companion walked around the front of the car and came over to the window. He wore a light jacket, camo pants, and a dark blue baseball cap that had a bunch of letters on it that from his angle, Jonah couldn't quite make out.

"Irish, huh?" he said, staring in through the window. He looked over at Klaus. "How about you? You Irish too?"

Klaus shook his head. "No. I'm from Dusseldorf."

The man looked disappointed, like he'd missed out on having his very own Irish buddy. It was time to move the conversation along.

"Listen, lads," Jonah said. "The reason we stopped yis is we're looking to find a gun store. Yesterday me and the missus got into a spot of bother. Things are getting dangerous here." He pointed at the men's rifles. "Don't suppose you know where we can find a couple of them, do yeh?" Then he pointed at the handguns they wore by their waists. "And maybe some of those jobbies too?"

The two men looked at each other and broke out into broad grins. The man whose great great granddaddy hailed from Skibereen said to Jonah, "Oh, I think we can help you out there, all right."

***

Twenty minutes later, Jonah pulled into a small strip mall off the Osceola Parkway and slotted the Taurus into a parking spot outside a single story building on the corner. In big red letters, on a garish yellow awning, it said: GUNS. He smiled to himself. That's what he was talking about.

In the back seat were Bill O'Shea and Darren Parker, who had brought them there. Turned out it was where the two men had gotten their own weapons only thirty minutes earlier. They had just returned from the gun store, parked their car, and were heading back to their hotel when Jonah stopped them.

The two were from Philadelphia. They'd come to Orlando as part of a group of fourteen on a fishing trip, and had been the only two to survive. Stocked up with weapons, ammo, and food, they were just about to head back to Philadelphia. Jonah was grateful the two friends were prepared to delay their trip in order to help him and Klaus out.

Bill was in construction, not the military, and his friend Darren was a fireman. Both had extensive weapons training, however, a relief to Jonah. They would be able to help match the right ammunition to the right gun, something he had been a little worried about.

A set of steel shutters covered both the store entrance and the windows to either side. Getting out of the car, Bill and Darren led the two around the corner where, amid a pile of rubble, was a gaping hole in the sidewall. Parked next to it was a John Deere front loader, its bucket lowered parallel to the ground.

Bill grinned at them. "Like I said, I'm in construction."

Inside the store, he asked Jonah, "You any idea what you're looking for exactly?"

Jonah pulled out a neatly folded sheet of paper from his back pocket. "Let's see now…" he said, opening it up. "I'm looking for a nine mil or a .45. Something easy to handle. I'll also need an AR-15 rifle of some description. I want one chambered for 5.56 NATO rounds with preferably a thirty round magazine. If there's any hunting rifles, I'll take one of them too. A Remington 700 would be nifty."

Bill looked at him approvingly. "I see you're a man who knows his weapons. That's going to improve your chances of survival dramatically."

"Eh, not exactly," Jonah said sheepishly. "The missus put the list together. She's been reading a lot of that post-apocalyptic fiction lately."

Bill looked impressed. "She must be some lady."

"Oh, that she is. Now regarding the pistol. I'm looking for a Glock, or a…a Sick Sewer," Jonah continued, scrunching his face up at Colleen's handwritten notes.

"A Sig Sauer," Darren corrected him. "I think that's what your missus is referring to."

"Yeh, that's it." Jonah tutted. "For such a smart girl, Colleen's writing is woeful. It's like the bleedin' cat wrote this."

The two Americans began searching the store for the required weapons, Jonah and Klaus in tow. Pulling out a pistol from a smashed display case, Bill handed it to Jonah. "I recommend something like this, a Glock 21. It's chambered in .45 ACP and got a helluva punch. Trust me, whatever you hit is going to stop dead in its tracks."

Jonah took the weapon, inspecting it.

"Nice thing is," Bill explained, "it's real easy to handle. See? There's no safety you need to fuck around with."

Jonah frowned. "No safety? Are yeh having me on?" Looking to either side of the pistol frame, a puzzled expression came over his face.

Bill laughed. "Glocks don't have manual thumb safeties like traditional pistols; they use a trigger safety instead. When we're done here, we'll go outside and do some target practice. I'll show you a suitable firing stance for both a handgun and a rifle. Also how to load your weapons correctly. How does that sound?"

"Magic!" Jonah exclaimed giddily, waving the Glock about like an excited schoolboy. "I tell yeh, I'm gagging to fire off this baby."

Bill gently pushed Jonah's arm to one side. "Easy there, fellah. First thing we better teach you is gun safety. We don't want the wrong people getting hurt, now do we?"

CHAPTER 13

Sitting behind the wheel of his brand new Toyota Tacoma, Cody drove west out of Knoxville on I-40. His Kimber 1911 was on his lap, the butt of the Ruger SR jammed into the passenger foot space, its muzzle facing away from him. Hitched to the back of the pickup, he towed an eighteen-foot travel trailer. His new home.

He passed the sign for the Holiday Inn and got into the right lane, then took the next exit ramp. A mile farther, he reached North Cedar Bluff junction and slowed to a stop. Pete pulled up behind him in the exact same model pickup, only Pete's Taco was blue, not desert tan like Cody's. Bringing up the rear, Walter drew up in a more upmarket white Tundra. It had been the last one left at the Toyota showroom, and Cody and Pete had both insisted he take it.

Cody swung left onto Cedar Bluff and drove under the I-40 underpass. After two hundred yards, he took a left onto North Peters Road and headed for the Guardian Armory. It was the rendezvous point he'd agreed with Chris the other day. It seemed as good a place as any, and was a chance for both groups to pick up more weapons and ammunition. Walter in particular needed to rearm, seeing as Mason had disarmed him at the gas station.

When they'd gotten home the previous evening, Walter had grilled him further on Chris. Cody told him what little he knew about him in such a short space of time.

He'd met him and his group at Dick's Sporting store, not far from the armory where, just like him, they'd been stocking up on camping supplies. Chris was in his late thirties. About five ten, muscular, with short blond hair, he'd told Cody that he'd been a senior executive at the movie theater chain, the Regal Entertainment Group, the only Knoxville-based company listed in the Fortune 1000. He had that vibe about him. Perhaps a little overbearing, he was supremely fit, with a confident demeanor. A typical alpha male. But he had integrity, and was not a thug like Mason, Cody reassured Walter again.

"I guess we'll see," Walter said when Cody finished. "It would be nice to find some like-minded people. With a bigger community, I can work on projects that are just not worth doing if there's only the three of us."

"Such as?"

"Such as building a settlement with proper infrastructure. Running water, electricity, plumbing, stuff like that."

Pete frowned. "That's pretty ambitious, Walter. What sort of power do you propose to use? Solar?"

"Maybe, though personally I prefer hydro. Build a settlement near a river and you can rig up a simple hydraulic pump too. Then not only do you have power, you got running water."

"You know how to do all that?" Cody asked.

"Sure, it's simple. For electricity, you just need to feed a pipe off the river and put a small turbine in it. It'll give you enough juice to run the house lights, charge batteries, stuff like that. Building a pump is straightforward enough."

"Great, Chris is going to love that." Cody hesitated a moment. "To be honest, he's picky about who he allows into his group. When he learned I was with two other people, he didn't seem too happy." Cody smiled at Walter. "He perked up when I told him you were a genius though."

They reached the Guardian Armory. Cody pulled into the large parking lot off Seven Oaks Drive and came to a stop about a hundred feet away from it. The gun shop was next to a karate dojo and a self-defense store. Like the previous day, it occurred to him how useless either martial arts or guns had been in protecting people against a deadly virus. For the survivors however, self-defense was becoming increasingly more necessary. Their encounter with Mason's gang the previous day had made that very clear.

Walter and Pete drew up to either side of him. Cody jumped out of the Tacoma and strolled across the lot to where Chris and his people sat on the steps outside the gun store. Twenty feet away was a line of four vehicles, a variety of different types of RVs. With eight in their group, they obviously planned on sharing accommodation. Cody was sure there was a reason for it. Perhaps Chris felt it was safer, or that it led to greater community spirit, or perhaps both.

Chris rose to his feet as Cody approached, and they shook hands. He looked over Cody's shoulder to where the three pickups sat parked. "Aren't your friends coming over?" he asked with a frown.

After his experience with Mason the other night, Walter wasn't taking any chances. He wanted to meet Chris away from everyone else first, rather than to walk up to a larger, well-armed group. The arrangement was that Cody would ask Chris to come over and meet Walter. Cody was a little dubious of the plan, in particular about how Chris might react. One way or the other, he was about to find out.

"Do you mind coming over to meet Walter by yourself?" he asked. "We ran into a little trouble yesterday. It's made him kind of cautious."

Chris looked at him curiously. "What kind of trouble?"

"The kind that leaves you with a bullet in your leg."

Chris stared over at Walter, who had gotten out of his pickup. He leaned against the hood and was looking in their direction. "Sure, I can do that," Chris said after a moment of evaluation. He turned to a man named Eddy who Cody had met the previous day as well. Chris's second in command, as far as he could tell. "Eddy, you guys stay here. I'm going over to introduce myself to Cody's friends."

A scowl came over Eddy's face. "Chris, they're joining us, not the other way around. They should get their asses over here and quit pansying around."

"I'll stay behind with Eddy and let you two talk if you like," Cody volunteered, anxious not to let doubt or suspicion enter what should be a friendly meeting between like-minded survivors.

Chris put his arm around Cody's shoulder. "It's okay, Ed. I trust Cody. Come on. Let's go."

The two walked across the lot and headed over to Walter. "Looks like you got yourselves some nice accommodation," Chris commented as they got closer.

Earlier that morning at the Tennessee RV Supercenter outside Knoxville, the three had picked out their travel trailers. On Walter's instructions, they'd selected lightweight, easy to tow vehicles. They needed to stay mobile. A forty-foot model, like the one Pete had first chosen, with every imaginable luxury inside, wasn't going to cut it tearing down a forest track at fifty miles an hour with a bunch of bloodthirsty bandits on their tails.

Reluctantly, Pete had downscaled to a less fancy model, a nineteen-foot Venture Sonic Lite. Cody chose a KZ Sportsmen Classic, while Walter picked out a Forest River Micro Lite. Pleased with their "purchases", they'd hitched them up to their trucks and driven back to Knoxville.

Chris strode ahead of Cody to Walter's pickup, his hand extended. Walter pushed himself off the bonnet and stuck out his hand out as well.

"Hey, Walter, I'm Chris. Shit, Cody wasn't kidding," he said, staring down at the bandage wrapped around

Walter's calf, where he'd cut away the lower portion of the trouser leg. "You in pain, buddy?"

"Nah, it's only a superficial wound. It'll heal soon." He looked down at the pistol holstered on Chris's right hip. "Got yourself a nice handgun there. Looks like a Steyr. Would I be right?"

Chris looked impressed. "You know your guns. Yep, it's a Steyr M9-A1. I legally own it. Got the paperwork to prove it too."

Walter smiled. "A guy named Mason currently has my legally-owned handgun. He's not exactly the nicest guy in the world."

"That the guy who shot you?"

Walter nodded. "He's the leader of a gang in east Knoxville. Soon there'll be more and more groups like his, safety in numbers and all that. Human nature dictates that not all of them will be nice people."

Chris pointed back across the lot. "I got a group of my own right here. Haven't known any of them long, but they're good people. I feel comfortable taking them into the hills with me. If you want to ride in our convoy, you guys are welcome to join us. Seeing as we just met, it's probably best you remain separate from our group for the moment, but there's no reason why we can't all ride out together, even set up camp next to one another."

Walter's shoulders relaxed. It appeared Chris's energy and enthusiasm had disarmed him, along with the fact Chris wasn't trying to railroad him into his gang. "That's kind of you to offer. I think we'll take you up on it. Where do you plan on heading exactly?"

"We're driving down to Lake Ocoee, it's part of the Cohutta Wilderness Area. There's a place called Wasson Lodge on the southwest shore. I took my wife and children there several times. The lake is full of fish, and there's deer and wild boar in the forest. It's about as perfect a spot as you could imagine."

Walter winked at Cody. "How about that? Just so happens we were heading in that direction too. It would be kind of dumb if we didn't all head off there together, wouldn't it?"

CHAPTER 14

Standing next to a small field outside the town of Benton, Tennessee, Sheriff John Rollins leaned against the door of his Dodge Charger watching a bulldozer shovel the last of the earth into a recently excavated pit. The huge pit constituted a mass grave of over a thousand people. Also scattered around the field were smaller individual graves where Benton's survivors had buried family members, erecting simple wooden crosses to mark them.

One week ago, the tiny agricultural town in Polk County, located along the northwestern fringe of the Cohutta Wilderness Area, had a population of approximately fourteen hundred people. Today, the count stood at thirty-seven. Seventeen men, fifteen women, and five children, with another four hundred unaccounted for, presumed to have left Benton in search of medical treatment in the nearby cities of Cleveland and Chattanooga.

For the past two days, Rollins and a team of volunteers had been clearing out houses one street at a time, loading the corpses into the back of a tarpaulin truck and hauling them up to the gravesite.

Though perhaps a fruitless act, it signified compassion for those who had died, part of what it meant to be human. At that moment, Rollins didn't feel particularly human. Perhaps the sight of the huge pile of bodies with their grotesque blistered faces had something to do with that, or the fact that in one of the marked graves lay his thirty-two-year-old pregnant wife and two-year old daughter.

Driving south down Route 411, Rollins spotted a familiar dark blue Nissan Titan approaching. It belonged to Chief Deputy Ned Granger, only appointed by Rollins two days ago. The previous week, Rollins had been chief deputy himself. As the only surviving member of the Polk County Sheriff's department, he'd been quickly elected sheriff by Benton's surviving townsfolk. Just thirty-seven years old, under normal circumstances Rollins was too young to become a sheriff. These weren't normal circumstances.

Granger pulled up behind him and got out of the pickup. Walking over, he gazed out into the field. "That's a sight I never want to see again," he said grimly. Earlier that day, he had been among those disposing of the bodies.

Compared to Rollins's tall lean figure, Granger was short and stocky, with jowly bulldog features. A tough, uncompromising man who'd been a local businessman before the disaster, he'd served as a soldier in the first Gulf War. Solid and dependable, Rollins had selected him for those very reasons. It also helped that the two men had known each other for several years. A good understanding of each other's capabilities would be critical in these challenging times.

"Me neither," Rollins replied. "Can't say they got much of a burial, but at least they got something."

Granger nodded. "We're done with the dead, time to focus on the living. Speaking of which…we got problems."

A couple of hours ago, Rollins had sent Granger north on a scouting trip in search of a good location for the Benton survivors. They needed to claim land where there was good hunting and fresh water.

"All right," Rollins said slowly. "Hit me with it. What gives?"

Granger drew his breath. "The dam is taken. Survivors from Chattanooga and Cleveland have claimed it.

There's about a half-dozen groups up there. They've occupied both sides of the river mouth and made it plain no one else is welcome."

"Damn," Rollins cursed under his breath.

While the Benton survivors had been burying their dead, others had been getting on with things. The hydroelectric dam at the mouth of the Ocoee River was an excellent location, with good land to either side and easy access to Route 74. West led to Cleveland City and Chattanooga, while the eastern route followed the northern shores of Lake Ocoee all the way to the far side of the Cohutta.

"How about Austral?" Rollins asked. Farther north, at the mouth of the Hiwassee River, the town of Austral was their next favored location.

Granger shook his head.

A sense of unease ran through Rollins. The good spots were going fast.

Unclipping the recently-scavenged radio handset from his belt, he raised it up to his mouth. Without power, the digital dispatch system at the sheriff's office no longer functioned, and with reports of prowling gangs in the area, it was vital he maintained good communications with his four deputies.

"Bravo Five, this is Bravo One. Do you read me? Over," he said, holding down the talk button. "Bravo Five, where are you, Hank?" he added, knowing that some of his newly-appointed deputies still hadn't got used to their assigned handles.

"Read you loud and clear, Sheriff," Henry Perter's voice came through a moment later. *"I'm back in Benton."* Unlike their police radios, on their five-watt handsets the range in which they could communicate wasn't more than a couple of miles.

"What's the situation at Camp Ocoee? Over."

An hour ago, Rollins had dispatched Perter in the opposite direction to Granger, to the YMCA adventure camp on the southwest shore of Lake Ocoee, another potential resettlement location on his list. After Granger's report, he feared the worst and held his breath while he waited for his deputy to reply.

"It's a real ugly scene. There's dead children everywh—"

"Hank, is the camp occupied or not?" Rollins cut in, his nerves getting to him. "I need the answer right away."

There was a moment's delay, then, *"Nobody there but the dead, Sheriff."*

Rollins breathed a sigh of relief. "How about Wasson Lodge?" he asked. Part of the overall YMCA complex, the lodge was a smaller family-oriented building that private groups rented out during the summers.

"Nope. It's unoccupied too."

"Thank God for that," Granger muttered, standing beside Rollins. "We need to get down there right away."

Rollins nodded. "Hank, get back there right now. When you reach the camp driveway, park your car across it and don't let anyone through. Camp Ocoee is our designated location. We need to hold it."

There was a moment's hesitation. *"I'll be on my own, John. What if somebody starts shooting at me?"*

"Then shoot right back. That's why I issued you that AR-15," Rollins told him curtly. Along with getting several radio handsets, Rollins and Granger had spent time at a gun store in Cleveland the other day too. "You'll have support soon. We'll be there in fifteen minutes. Over and out."

Rollins managed to raise one more of his two other deputies, instructing her to head to the camp as well. The Benton survivors were staking their claim. Camp Ocoee now officially belonged to them.

Rollins checked his watch. "Well, Ned, looks like we've found our new home. Instruct the group to start moving out."

He opened the door to the Charger, slid behind the wheel and started the engine. Driving south, he headed for Camp Ocoee. Though relieved his group had found somewhere to relocate, something told Rollins things would get a lot worse before they got better.

CHAPTER 15

The convoy of seven vehicles drove out of the parking lot and back onto Seven Oaks Drive. When they reached I-40 they headed west, navigating around the abandoned cars that littered the highway. They'd either run dry or their occupants had succumbed to vPox. Acting as pacemaker, Walter took the lead. As a soldier who'd served in Iraq, he knew all about roadside ambushes, and Chris had allowed him to organize the convoy's security arrangements.

That morning, he'd picked up a set of three Motorola 2-way radio handsets at a Walmart. On discovering that Chris's team didn't have any, he'd reached into the cabin of his pickup and pulled out an identical set.

"Here, a present," he said with a quick grin, handing the box to Chris. "Not the best comms in the world, but all I could find on short notice."

The three spent the next few minutes configuring the radios to the same channel number and privacy code. Though advertising a range of thirty miles, the reality was that because of obstructions such as trees, hills, and buildings, the five-watt radios wouldn't work over more than two or three miles. The sets had earbuds, however, that allowed hands-free Push-To-Talk usage, and Walter had picked up car phone chargers for them too.

Riding shotgun with him, armed with an AK-47 rifle, sat Tim, an overweight man in his fifties who'd assured Walter before they left that he was "weapons trained."

The second most important position in the convoy was the trailing vehicle, which Cody volunteered to take up. Chris had assigned Eddy to ride with him. It was important to have their best shooters at both the front and back of the convoy.

Cody was also well-armed. Before leaving the gun store, he'd stocked up on extra supplies. As well as additional ammunition, in a shiny new holster by his right hip was his Kimber 1911, and on the other side, in a leather sheath, a seven-inch hunting knife he'd gotten at Dick's the previous day. Behind him on the back seat, and within easy reach, was his Ruger SR.

Driving at fifty miles an hour, the group soon reached the junction with I-75 and took the southbound exit for Chattanooga. An hour later, they approached a town called Cleveland, where they turned east onto Route 74 and headed for the town of Ocoee. There, they would turn onto Hwy 411 before finally heading into the Cohutta.

Though they'd brought physical maps with them, Cody switched on the Taco's onboard GPS system and checked their progress.

"That's not going to work," Eddy said in a surly tone. "In case you didn't know, we're in the middle of an apocalypse."

Eddy was a gruff, stocky man in his thirties who didn't exactly exude friendliness. So far, other than some small talk, the two hadn't said much on the journey. Cody hoped Eddy knew how to use the LAR-15 semiautomatic rifle resting against the passenger door, because other than that, he would have preferred to travel on his own.

"The satellites are still functioning," he told him. "Problem is, after a few weeks they lose their accuracy. They need to be regularly updated by the ground monitoring stations. Still, they shouldn't be too off yet."

"Yeah? How do you know that?"

"Walter told me." Cody squinted down at the screen. "We're eight miles west of Ocoee. That sound right to you?"

Eddy bent over and checked the map. "Yeah, that's about right," he said grudgingly.

For the next couple of miles neither of them spoke. "What did you do before the vPox?" Cody asked, breaking the silence.

"I worked in construction," Eddy replied. "I'm a carpenter. That's how come Chris invited me to join him. Along with the fact I have firearms training."

"Were you in the military?"

"Nah, the shooting range mainly. A little hunting too."

"That's good. My dad taught me how to hunt in the Blue Ridge Mountains, not too far from where we're going. I'm a pretty good shot."

Eddy gave Cody a dead fish stare. "That right?"

"Yeah," Cody replied, trying not to let his temper show.

Keeping his eyes on the road, his thoughts drifted back to his father and how, being a soldier, he'd gotten Cody interested in guns and all things military from an early age. After he left the family and went back to Greenville, the small North Carolina town he was from, Cody hadn't seen much of him. Once or twice a year, though, he'd take him on hiking trips into the Chattahoochee Mountains west of Greenville.

On those trips, his father had taught him how to hunt, so long as he swore he never told his mother that he'd been allowed to handle weapons. Cody's mom didn't take too kindly to him being around guns, which he always thought was funny seeing she married a military man.

Cody was a thirteen-year-old boy and loved them, though, and took to shooting like a duck to water. His father told him he had a good eye, fast reflexes, and that he'd make a fine soldier someday. Later, in the evenings when they'd set up camp and his father took to the whiskey, he'd take it back and make Cody swear that he would never enlist, that a soldier's life was cursed and they had to do the bidding of reptiles. Whenever Cody asked who the reptiles were, his father would let out a bitter laugh and say, "The politicians of course. Lower than a snake's belly, each and every one of them."

Five years later, when he got sent to prison for robbing a liquor store, drunk out of his mind, Cody's mother discouraged Cody from visiting him. At the time, he obeyed her wishes. Later, when he'd overcome his shame about what his father had become, he felt guilty. Maybe if he'd visited him, his father wouldn't have checked into that roach motel outside Greenville a week after his release, put the muzzle of his Kimber 1911 special under his chin, and blown the back of his skull off.

Turned out, he willed Cody that gun. It was why he had it today. Some people thought that was creepy. Cody didn't. He was proud to own it. His father put his life on the line to serve his country. It killed him in the end, the slow way, but he did it all the same. He was a true patriot.

Clocking up the miles, Cody resumed his conversation with Eddy.

"How about the rest of your group? What sort of backgrounds do they come from?" he asked.

"All sorts. Tim, the guy riding with Walter, had some type of business, don't know what exactly. Liz is a botanist, used to work in the Department of Agriculture south of downtown. Greta, the tall girl, kinda bossy—she's a nurse. Mark worked in a warehouse, and James is a mechanic. Don't think you've talked to either of them yet."

Neither of the two had said a word when Cody first met the group the previous day. "How about Emma?" he asked. "You know what she used to do?"

Eddy shook his head. "Nope."

Startlingly pretty, with long brown hair and green eyes, Emma was around Cody's age. After spending an hour with the group the previous day, he'd noted she didn't appear to have a boyfriend. Driving home afterward, he realized why someone so pretty was unattached. No doubt, a week earlier, she did have someone in her life, but with a huge kill rate (ninety-eight percent of those exposed to the virus, according to Chris), vPox had put a stop to that. Things had changed so fast his mind hadn't yet caught up with all the implications of the new reality everyone found themselves in.

For the first time, he saw Eddy smile. "Maybe Chris brought her along because she's hot." He grinned at Cody. "It's all right. Now that civilization's bit the dust, we can say shit like that again."

A few minutes later, they reached the outskirts of Ocoee. There was a crackle of static, then Walter's voice came over the radio. *"Attention group, this is Knox One. There's an Exxon station coming up on our right. I'm pulling in there, over."*

Ocoee would be their last stop before heading up to Wasson Lodge about fifteen miles farther on. If the lodge was occupied, they intended to find somewhere else suitable along the lake shore.

A moment later, Chris responded. *"Copy that Knox One, this is Knox Leader. See you in a few."*

Before leaving Knoxville, Chris had issued call signs to the six vehicles assigned radios. Walter and Cody had exchanged wry smiles when Chris named himself "Knox Leader". He'd made sure to leave no doubt in anyone's mind who was in charge.

Cody picked up his radio off the seat divider. Pushing down the PTT button, he said, "Knox Six to group, copy that. Over and out."

A few minutes later, they pulled off the highway and into the service station. Being the last to arrive, he had to park at the far end of the forecourt, along the sidewall of a small McDonald's outlet.

"Boy, I could kill a quarter pounder with cheese right now. Along with some fries and a Coke," he said, cutting the engine.

Eddy grunted. "Me and you both."

Cody got out of the pickup and walked over to where Walter and Chris stood by the pumps. Walter had his bag of tricks out, a similar set to the one he'd used back at the Chevron station: a pump, a length of hose, and a battery-powered drill.

"We better fill up before heading into the mountains," Walter said as Cody approached. "Who knows when others figure out how to access the underground tanks?"

"What's the drill for?" Chris asked, anxious to learn exactly how Walter rigged up his system.

"It gets attached to the pump. Quickest way to run it," Water replied. He grinned. "Otherwise, you end up with a sore arm."

At that moment Tim ambled over, carrying a couple of five-gallon jerry cans in each hand.

"You guys need a hand?" Cody asked. That morning he, Walter, and Pete had already filled several gas cans themselves and stored them in the backs of their trailers.

Chris shook his head. "It's okay. Walt's going to show me and Tim how he puts this system together."

"My name is Walter," Walter corrected him. "Nobody calls me Walt."

Leaving them to it, Cody strolled over to the store. He had a mind to pick up some snacks, also some gum. Things like that wouldn't last forever.

The entrance had already been busted open. Without any power, it was dark inside, and it felt a little spooky as he walked up to the counter. Somewhere on his right, there was the sound of rustling, then something clattered onto the floor. Cody whipped out his Kimber. "Who's there?" he said nervously.

A face peered out from around a row of shelves. It was Emma.

"Oh, it's you," he said, relieved. He slipped the Kimber back in its holster.

"Kinda jumpy, aren't you?" Emma asked, smiling softly.

"In my experience, gas stations can be dangerous places. Walter nearly got himself killed in one the other day."

Emma's face dropped. "Oh, sorry…I didn't know that."

Cody waved a hand. "That's all right. You seen the snacks rack? I'm hankering for some potato chips."

Emma laughed. "Me too! That's why I came in here." She indicated for him to follow her, and the two walked up to the counter where, on one side, a large display rack contained every imaginable snack food. Cody grabbed two packs of Grandma Utz chips and handed one to Emma. Popping them open, they leaned against the counter, eating them.

"Mmmm, BBQ flavor…my favorite," Emma said. "I'm going to be so upset when stuff like this is all gone."

"Me too." Cody grinned. "How about we grab the rest of them on our way out? We'll hide them somewhere. It'll be our little secret."

"You're so bad," Emma giggled.

"What did you do before the vPox," Cody asked. "Were you in college?" He was pretty sure Emma hadn't been at UTK. He would have remembered her face.

"I was a pharma sales rep for GlaxoSmithKline. My job was to persuade doctors to prescribe our company's drugs to their patients. I never felt comfortable doing it. It felt so phony, especially once I knew the reason for promoting most products. It was always about the bottom line, not patient welfare. Still, it paid the rent. How about you?"

"I'd just finished my third year at UTK, studying history. To be honest, I didn't really enjoy it. It wasn't what I was expecting when I enrolled in the course."

"Really? Why not?"

Cody hesitated. "I found it dull as hell. I always loved history at school. Especially military history, you know, the Civil War, the two World Wars, Vietnam, all that stuff. The way we had to study it at college sucked all the fun out of it for me. All those stories I'd enjoyed reading became dry term papers I was forced to churn out with citations and footnotes. So tedious." He grinned. "Guess I wasn't cut out for academic life. I've always been more of a practical guy. Just like my father. He was a military man."

"I see. Did vPox take him away?"

Cody shook his head. "It took my mother and brother. My father died before then." He changed the subject. "How about you? Any of your family survive?"

A haunted look came over Emma's face. "No, my whole family is gone. My mother, father, younger sister, and brother. I cared for them in my parents' house. One by one, they passed away. All the time I was certain I would be next. It just never happened."

"Same thing happened to me with my two roommates," Cody said quietly. "I feel bad I didn't get down to Phoenix to be with my mom and brother. Everything happened so fast. By the time I knew what was happening, it was too late."

He stopped speaking when someone came in through the doorway and strode up the aisle. It was Chris. To Cody's surprise, he had an angry look on his face.

"What the hell are you two doing here?" he said when he reached them, talking to them like they were naughty schoolchildren.

"Just talking…and eating." Cody raised his bag of chips. "Want some?"

Chris glowered at him. "No, I don't. You two need to come out and help with the refueling. It's selfish to stand around and let everyone else do the work."

Cody felt his temper rise and was tempted to tell him that he'd just offered to help five minutes ago. That if it took more than three people to pour gasoline into a few cans, they were in real trouble. He thought better of it though and, pushing themselves off the counter, the two followed Chris out of the store.

Reaching the doorway, Emma nudged Cody. "Chris has been getting kinda possessive about me lately," she whispered. "I really don't like it."

Cody raised an eyebrow, but didn't reply. Perhaps Eddy's earlier jest had some validity to it after all. With her sultry looks and outgoing yet warm personality, Chris had obviously taken a shine to Emma. Cody couldn't blame him. So had he.

CHAPTER 16

At the YMCA staff lounge, Sheriff Rollins sat at the table. To either side of him were his recently sworn-in deputies: Ned Granger, Henry Perter, Bert Olvan, and Mary Sadowski, that comprised the five-man Benton Survivors Group Council. The council, quickly established by Rollins and Granger, was responsible for all decision-making at the camp, and their ruling was final. Perhaps it wasn't the finest example of democracy at work, but it did maintain law and order. Right now, that was more important.

There was a satisfied look on Rollins's face. Despite the unpleasant task of having to bury yet more decomposing bodies, most of them children, everything had gone according to plan, and all afternoon he and his team had assisted the other thirty-two Benton survivors in moving out of town and up to the lakeside camp.

Camp Ocoee had over twenty buildings in total, and there was plenty of room for everyone. There were family cabins, several dorms, an infirmary, a large dining hall, as well as a chapel, an arts and crafts room, and some other recreational facilities. At the heart of the camp was a square lawn around which the administrative cabins were centered.

Since arriving, Rollins had made several changes to security arrangements. He'd moved the original roadblock

Henry Perter had manned down to the junction of the Cookson Creek Road. It prevented anyone arriving from the north from driving past the YMCA camp and on to Wasson Lodge, located nearby. Simultaneously, he'd set up a second roadblock farther south, stopping anyone approaching from a southerly direction.

In essence, he'd expanded the amount of territory his group now controlled. The last thing they needed were unruly neighbors occupying the lodge. It was less than a mile away from their camp.

"All right, Hank," he said to Perter, "open the map. Let's get on with the planning."

Tall and narrow-shouldered, with a humorous but slightly nervous disposition, Henry Perter was in his fifties and a friend of Granger's from before. In front of him was a U.S. Forest Service map of the area. Earlier, he'd found a stack of them in the office cabin. Opening it up, he spread it out on the table and the five peered at it from all sides.

Rollins pulled out a Biro from the top pocket of his shirt and marked the two spots where he'd set up the roadblocks. "For now, we need to keep these running 24/7. From now on, let's call them 'checkpoints'. Sounds friendlier," he added with a dry smile. "With more and more people leaving the cities, we have to be ready for all eventualities. I've already assigned which men will be on duty tonight, but from tomorrow on, we'll need a proper roster. Mary, can I leave you in charge of that?"

Mary Sadowski nodded. A small, wiry woman in her sixties, she'd been a clerk at the Polk County Courthouse for the past thirty years. Rollins had known her a long time and knew just how efficient she was. "They'll need proper training," she said, making a note in the legal pad in front of her in her neat efficient writing. "Who's going to give them that?"

Rollins smiled. "Why, you of course. Select all men and women over the age of eighteen. No exceptions." He glanced across the table at Granger sitting opposite him. "Tomorrow morning, Ned will train the trainer."

Granger gave Sadowski a friendly wink. "How good are you with a handgun, Mary?"

In reply, the courthouse clerk reached down and pulled a Sig Sauer nine millimeter pistol from her waist holster. "See this? Been my personal weapon of choice for ten years. I've fired it many times."

"How about a rifle?"

"That too. I go to the shooting range twice a month. Used to, that is," she corrected herself.

Granger nodded approvingly. "Guard duty is mostly about staying alert. It's our advanced warning on anything coming our way, so good communication procedures are vital. Don't get me wrong, everyone needs to know how to fire a weapon too. The checkpoints are our first line of defense."

"Won't two people standing by a vehicle be vulnerable to attack?" Bert Olvan asked doubtfully. He was a big man with a large belly and a bushy beard who'd owned a small construction company prior to the pandemic. "I mean, if somebody is going to try and take this place, it's going to be more than just one person."

"Absolutely," Rollins agreed. "Tomorrow, we'll start building proper defenses. For now, a truck parked across the road will have to do. The most important thing is that the guards radio in immediately if they spot any strangers in the area. Like Ned said, communication is the key thing."

Rollins wasn't a military man, but he was a quick thinker. What he'd originally perceived as a weakness in the camp's location, he now saw as one of its strengths. The camp was on a large piece of headland that jutted out into the lake, and was surrounded on three sides by water. It meant that if they were overrun by a larger force, they would be trapped. However, on further reflection, he realized two things. First, with only one roadway into the camp that came in from the west, it would be easier to defend. Secondly, if they were overrun, the lake could actually provide a means of escape by which their attackers couldn't follow, so long as they made the correct preparations.

"It's not just the driveway we need to defend," he continued. "Anyone attacking the camp will most likely come through the woods where it'll be harder to spot them." On the map, he pointed out two narrow inlets north and south of the headland that formed a half-open pincer shape. He drew a line on the map, connecting the two inlets. "If attackers try coming through the forest, this right here provides us with the shortest line to defend. Agreed?"

Everyone at the table nodded their heads in agreement.

Ned Granger spoke up. "Problem is, John, that's real thick forest. Without posting guards every ten yards, it'll be easy to sneak past. Especially at night. We'll need to run tripwire. Something that gives us a warning. Perhaps, in time, even create a clearcut. That'll make it easier to spot intruders."

"How about digging a trench with sharpened stakes at the bottom?" Perter suggested mischievously. "That'll learn 'em."

Rollins grinned. "All in time, Hank. For now, tripwire." He looked around the table. "Before finishing up on security, there's one other thing we need to discuss. Not to be pessimistic, but we need to draw up emergency plans for an evacuation in case we get overrun by a larger force. Bert, how many boats we got here?"

Earlier, Rollins had requested that Olvan take a look and see what the situation was at the camp regarding boats. He knew that water sports and fishing had played a big role in the camp's activities.

"Me and Hank went down to the boathouse and found two skiffs inside," Olvan said. "Not enough for thirty-seven people, so we hauled in another four from private homes around the area, making six in total. They're all sixteen-footers or bigger, so that ought to do it."

"What size motors do they have?" Mary Sadowski asked. "If we leave in a hurry, they need to be fast."

"We got four sixty-horsepower engines. They'll do about thirty miles an hour," Olvan replied. "The other two are smaller. We're going to see about getting them replaced tomorrow."

"Excellent," Rollins said, pleased. "Next thing. If we need to evacuate the camp, which direction do we head?" He jabbed a finger at the northernmost area of the headland. "If we place the boats in this little cove right here, we can head north to the dam…uh…where the good folk of Chattanooga will be waiting to greet us with open arms."

A chuckle went around the table.

Northeast of the camp, across a wide strait, was a long channel of water. Rollins ran his finger along it. "Or, before reaching the dam, we could head east along the Indian Creek Inlet. Right at the end is the 302."

A twisting, winding road, Route 302 ran west to east, following the contour of Lake Ocoee's southern shoreline before it turned sharply south and headed down to the Georgia state line.

Granger looked doubtful. "That's the long way round to get to the 302, John. I say we take the boats down to the south headland." He trailed a finger to where the lake narrowed into the shape of a twisted tail. The area was marked as Baker Creek Inlet. "We can reach the 302 here too, only quicker. We could even set up an emergency camp there, hide a few pickups and jeeps in the forest. It's not like we're short on vehicles."

"That's a better idea," Rollins said, studying the map carefully. He looked around the table. "Are we all good with that?" Everyone nodded their heads in agreement. "All right, south it is. Let's just hope this is a plan we never need to execute."

"For sure," Henry Perter said. "Still, in life you got to have a Plan B. You never know what's coming up next. If we didn't know that last week, we sure as hell know it now."

"All right, next on the agenda is food and water," Rollins said, staring down at his checklist. "After that, we need to discuss what we can do about power. We've got a diesel generator that'll do us for now, but we can't rely on it forever. Eventually, fuel is going run out."

Perter frowned. "That's going to be tough. Perhaps we can scavenge solar panels somewhere around here."

"Hank, we got a ton of rivers here. I think a water turbine is better," Olvan cut in. "Or maybe our Chattanooga friends can get the dam working and we can trade them something for running a line over here."

"How about squirrel pelts?" Perter suggested. "You think they'll go for that?"

Rollins chuckled. "All right, let's talk about water and food. That's more important right now. Mary, where do we stand on that?"

"Everything is under lock and key at the dining hall," Mary replied. I've made a full inventory of—"

Rollins's radio, which sat on the table in front of him, crackled to life. *"Bravo Base, this is Cookson Papa North. Do you read me? Over."*

Rather than using individual's call signs, Rollins had named the two checkpoints Cookson Papa North and Cookson Papa South, making their identification immediate. He picked up the radio. "Copy that, Papa North. This is Bravo One, over."

"Sheriff, a convoy of seven vehicles has just arrived here. They're demanding access to Wasson Lodge. You better get down here right away."

Rollins eyes widened. *Seven vehicles?* That spelled trouble. Around the table, all four of his deputies had already stood and picked up their rifles resting against the wall in a neat line. As well as retrieving his own weapon, Granger grabbed Rollins's too.

"Hang tight, Papa North. We'll get down there right away."

As he exited the room, Rollins barked out orders over his radio for a response team to head down to the Cookson Road junction, thankful that he'd had the sense to reconfigure the checkpoints when he first arrived at the camp. Otherwise, at this very moment, a group of seven vehicles would be rolling past them to occupy Wasson Lodge.

If his team didn't get down there soon, the newly-arrived group might just do that anyway.

CHAPTER 17

After gassing up, the convoy pulled out of the Exxon station. Walter's white Tundra remained in the lead, though this time, Cody slotted in behind him while another member of Chris's group took up the rear. Almost immediately, the southbound exit for Route 411 came up on their right. It would take them to Ocoee town, where they would come off the highway and head up to the lake.

"What did Chris want with you back there?" Eddy asked curiously after Cody made the turn onto the 411. "He looked pissed coming out of the store."

Cody hesitated a moment before speaking. "He told us that me and Emma weren't pulling our weight."

Eddy let out a low chuckle. "Maybe he was making sure you two weren't pulling your clothes off in there. He's got a thing for her."

"Yeah, I'm picking up on that." Cody shrugged. "None of my business though."

Eddy gave him a look. "I'd keep it that way too, if I was you."

There wasn't much to the town of Ocoee. This was a pleasant rural area with a low population even before the disaster, a mixture of farmland and thick forest to either side of the highway. They passed a small gas station, an agricultural feed store, a few smaller stores, then the post office. Around them, the streets were deserted. Cody didn't glimpse a single soul behind the curtains of any of the dwellings. vPox had taken out the town, like every other one in the country.

Approaching Steve's Pawn Shop, Walter slowed down, then turned onto Sloan's Gap Road, a winding country lane that, according to the map, would take them all the way to Wasson Lodge.

Back in Knoxville, Chris had described the lodge as an idyllic location. Built right on Lake Ocoee's shoreline, there were catfish and bass in the lake, trout in the nearby streams, wild boar and deer in the forest. Personally, Cody wouldn't have chosen to live somewhere with such a connection to his family, but everybody was wired differently. Perhaps it was a way of remembering them. Perhaps Chris planned on setting up a shrine for them. Who knew?

After passing through several miles of open farmland, they turned a long bend in the road and drove into deep forest where the hot June sun disappeared from view. Five minutes later, they reached the junction of Cookson Creek Road and turned right, following a sign for YMCA Camp Ocoee.

Walter slowed down, then came to a stop. Cody pulled up behind him.

"What's going on?" Eddy asked.

"Beats me." Cody poked his head out the window, but couldn't lean out far enough to see up ahead.

Walter's voice came over the radio. *"Knox One to group. We got a situation. There's a pickup truck parked across the road with two armed men standing behind it. They're preventing me from going any farther. I'm going to get out and see what gives. I'll keep the channel open so you can all hear me."*

"Wait up, Walt!" Chris's voice cut in. *"I'm coming with you. Everyone else remain in your vehicles and stay alert."*

There was the sound of a car door slamming. Before long, Chris strode past Cody, then disappeared from view as he walked along the side of Walter's trailer.

Next thing, Cody heard Chris's voice over Walter's open channel. *"All right, Walt. You see anyone else around other than these two guys?"*

There was a short sigh, then, *"Nope. That's it, as far as I can make out."*

"Okay, let's get over there. With twelve of us and only two of them, I don't see them delaying us long."

"I'm not so sure," Walter replied. *"My guess is they're part of a larger group that's taken over the YMCA camp, maybe the lodge too."*

"We'll find out soon enough," Chris said, his voice tense.

There was the sound of boots walking on the asphalt surface. Raising the volume on the radio so he could continue to listen, Cody opened his door and stepped out onto the road, then took a few paces out so he got a view of the road up ahead.

Fifty yards past Walter's truck, a red pickup was parked across the road. Behind it, two men stood, one on each side, both with semi-automatic rifles raised to their shoulders. When Walter and Chris got to within twenty feet, one of them lifted their hand.

"That's far enough," he said, his voice coming over clearly on Walter's radio.

"Let me do the talking," Chris murmured to Walter. "Okay mister, what gives here? Me and my people need to pass through. We're heading up to the lake."

"I'm sorry," a respectful but firm voice responded. "This road is off limits to strangers."

Chris placed his hands on his hips. "Says who, exactly?"

"Say the survivors of Benton, a town fifteen miles north of here. We've taken over the YMCA camp. No offense to you people, but we're not allowing strangers onto our property. There's plenty of other land around, like pretty much the whole country. I suggest you drive back to the highway and find someplace else to go."

Chris clearly wasn't ready to give up that easily, however. "How about Wasson Lodge?" he asked. "Have you taken that over too?"

"Nope. But we don't want any strangers there. It's too close to our camp."

Even from a distance of fifty yards, Cody could see Chris thrust his jaw out. "See, I got eleven armed people with me. You sure you're in a position to stop us?"

The edge to his voice had grown hard. Chris was someone who obviously didn't like to back down. Cody didn't appreciate his tone one bit, and doubted Walter did either. These were locals who had claimed the land first. They weren't keen on a large group of strangers moving onto their patch, and who could blame them?

"Mister, our group is bigger than yours," the guard growled, clearly irritated by Chris's demeanor. "In fact, here come some of them now. I've nothing more to say to you. You can talk to Sheriff Rollins."

A Dodge Charger with tan side markings and a flashing roof light drove out of a nearby side road. It pulled up twenty feet away and a man in a sheriff's uniform stepped out. Cody couldn't make out his features clearly but he looked tall and lean. Another man got out from the passenger side. He looked older, shorter, with a portly figure, dressed in regular clothes.

Behind the Charger, several more pickups pulled up. Men dressed in jeans and T-shirts spilled out of them, all armed with rifles. Some stayed behind the doors of their vehicles while others fanned out, seeking cover on either side of the tree-lined road.

The sheriff and his companion walked over to where the guards stood opposite Chris and Walter. "Hi, Sam," said the sheriff, approaching the guard who'd been doing all the talking. "What's going on here?"

"Afternoon, Sheriff. We got a group of seven vehicles looking to get up to the lake. This man here says he wants to occupy Wasson Lodge. I told him the territory is off limits, but he don't seem to hear me too good."

"Sam is correct," the sheriff said to Chris and Walter. "All land behind this checkpoint belongs to the Benton survivors. I'm afraid we're not allowing anyone through. There's plenty more land in the Cohutta, just not right here."

"Look, Sheriff," Chris said impatiently. "I brought my wife and family to Wasson Lodge on several occasions. I have a connection with the area. We're not bandits, we're good people. You won't have any problems with us."

"Sorry, I can't let you in," the sheriff said flatly.

"Come on, Chris. Let's go," Walter broke in. "We're wasting time. There's plenty of other places we can go."

"All right," Chris said in a surly tone, a man used to getting his own way. Cody could tell he was deeply unhappy how this was panning out.

"Sheriff, seeing as you're from around here, you got any suggestions where we should go?" Walter asked in a friendly tone. "We need somewhere close to a river where I can build my micro hydro."

Before leaving Knoxville, Walter had assembled the parts he needed for his pet project. When he'd opened up the back of his trailer to show him outside the Guardian Armory, Chris's eyes had lit up. Right away, he could see how useful Walter would be in building infrastructure for his new community.

"A micro hydro? What's that exactly?" the sheriff asked in a curious tone.

"It's a type of hydroelectric power," Walter told him. "I'm hoping to produce fifty-plus kilowatts from it. Enough to run house lights for our community, recharge batteries, run a fridge, that kind of thing. I just need to find a spot on a river with good water pressure."

"How long would it take you to build something like that?"

"Not long. I brought all the parts with me. I plan on building a water filtration system too. Later, I'll build storage tanks, so we can keep a regular supply of drinking water. Water is the first requirement of any survival situation, whether you're an individual or a community."

"How come you know all this stuff?" The sheriff's tone had become increasingly more interested.

"I was an Army combat engineer for seventeen years. Our battalion got sent on several humanitarian missions in South America and Africa. To be honest, I always felt a lot better building stuff rather than blowing it up."

"See?" Chris broke in. "I've put together a team of highly skilled people. I got a nurse, a carpenter, a botanist. If you like, I—"

"I got them all too," Rollins told him curtly. "One thing I don't have is a good engineer, someone who knows how to build infrastructure. All right, Mr. Engineer. Why don't you come around to this side of the vehicle and tell me what else seventeen years in an Army combat battalion taught you, and how we can use it in a situation like this."

CHAPTER 18

Russ Willis stood beside his Suzuki V-Strom 1000 and peeked his head around a bend on Cookson Creek Road, a pair of Steiner binoculars raised to his face. Three hundred yards away, at the end of the line of vehicles, a red pickup truck sat parked lengthways across the road, blocking the way. Behind it, a man armed with an assault rifle was in a discussion with Walter and another guy. A second armed guard stood looking on.

From the animated gestures Walter's companion was making, it looked like he was doing all the talking. The occasional shake of the guard's head told Russ that whatever he was asking for, he wasn't being granted. Presumably, to be allowed access up to the lake. Why else would the convoy have come off Route 411 and driven up this remote country road? It was the only thing that made sense.

"Come on, guys," Russ muttered disconsolately. "Let them through. I want to go home."

Tired and hungry, he was at least grateful for the liter bottle of water he'd managed to grab along the way after leaving Knoxville. He'd been following the group for over three hours now, and hoped they'd reached their final destination, then he could head back and give Mason the news.

The previous afternoon, after Walter and his friends had fled the Chevron station, Mason had sent Russ off in search of them, with instructions not to come back until he found them. Scouring the city, he saw no sign of them. Nor that morning, where for hours he'd traveled up and down the city's highways. Around 11 a.m., from an above overpass, he'd spotted a green Chevy Malibu hurtling west down Interstate 40.

"Dammit, I know that piece of shit!" he said excitedly, gazing through the Steiners. It was the same vehicle that, from out of nowhere, had driven down the back of the Chevron station and rescued Walter and his friend.

He'd ridden down from the overpass and trailed the Malibu. After a few miles it turned off the freeway and pulled into the parking lot of the city's main Toyota dealership on Parkside Drive. Watching from a discreet distance, he saw Walter get out of the front passenger seat. Then a tall, skinny kid with shoulder-length brown hair stepped out from behind the wheel. Russ was pretty sure it was the same one who'd saved Walter's ass the previous night. A moment later, Pete got out the back door.

"Hot damn!" he exclaimed. "Mason's gonna love me. I've found all three pieces of shit!"

Twenty minutes later, a white Tundra pickup and two Tacomas pulled out of the lot and headed back in the direction of the city. Next stop had been the Tennessee RV Supercenter, where a short time later the three vehicles emerged from the lot, each with a twenty-foot trailer in tow.

From there they had driven to the Guardian Armory. At the far side of the parking lot, Russ watched the three men meet up with a group of nine people. Three were women. One was a real looker, with dark, wavy hair, dressed in a T-shirt and tight-fitting jeans. Russ licked his lips. She had a hell of a figure.

Parked close by were two brand new pickups hitched up to trailers, also a couple of Winnebagos. It appeared the group was about to leave the city. That meant he would have to follow them to wherever they planned on going, otherwise he would lose them. Looked like he had a long day ahead of him.

Down at the roadblock, a cream and tan Dodge Charger suddenly appeared, coming out of a nearby junction. It pulled up behind the red pickup and two men stepped out. One wore a sheriff's uniform. Behind them, several other vehicles drew up, and men with semi-automatic rifles got out to take positions behind the trees to either side of the road.

After some discussion, Walter and his friend walked around the back of the pickup where they continued their talk with the sheriff and his friend. Finally, after what seemed like an interminable amount of time, a guard climbed into the red pickup and reversed back onto the margin of the road.

Shaking hands with the sheriff, Walter and his companion walked back to their vehicles. Moments later, Walter's truck drove past the roadblock, followed by the rest of the convoy. Once the last vehicle passed, the red pickup started its engine and drove across to block the road once more. Then the sheriff and his group got into their vehicles, turned around, and headed back up the side road, disappearing from view.

With a sigh of relief, Russ wheeled his V-Strom around. He started it up and headed back toward Route 411. Picking up speed, he took a sharp bend in the road. It was a hundred and twenty miles to Knoxville and he was anxious to get back as soon as possible. He couldn't wait to tell Mason the news.

CHAPTER 19

Back in the staff lounge, Sheriff Rollins sat with his deputies again. They were discussing their decision to allow the group from Knoxville to take over Wasson Lodge. Other than Mary Sadowski, all had agreed.

She sat at the table with a frown on her face. "The leader, Chris…he's trouble. I can see him causing all sorts of problems."

"Too much ego," Ned Granger agreed. "But he's no gangster. And his group is made up of regular people, not like some of the folk we've seen roaming around here."

"It's early days," Sadowski warned. "Let's see how they behave in a month's time. Remember, our group is made up of people we've known for years. I think we're taking a big risk."

"Mary, these days everything is a risk," Rollins said. "Look, we need someone like Walter to help build our infrastructure. He's a professional, a proper engineer. Also, it's a good idea to have allies close by. Who knows when we might need them?"

Sadowski sighed. "Well, it's done now. May I suggest we hurry up with our defenses in case our *allies* aren't as friendly as you think? We got a nice camp here. It's got to be a temptation." She looked around at the men. "Sorry, I hate to be the cynic around here. Just the way I am."

Rollins smiled briefly. "We wouldn't want you any other way." He checked his watch. "All right, let's move up the training schedule and start on things right away. Ned, you good for that, or you need more time to prepare?"

Granger shook his head. "No need. Mary and I can take a group of ten right now and begin weapons training. Tonight I'll draw up the plans for our defenses. Tomorrow we'll go fetch the materials and get to work. After that, we'll start running the drills. People need to be prepared for what to do if we ever come under attack."

"We should run nighttime drills too, as well as during the day," Olvan suggested. "That's when we're most likely to be hit."

"Absolutely," Granger agreed. "It's never going to be the same as the real thing, but preparation is everything. We need to make Camp Ocoee a place people think twice about trying to take over."

"Speaking of Camp Ocoee," Sadowski said, "I was thinking perhaps we ought to change the name to Camp Benton in memory of our old town."

"That's a nice idea," Rollins said. He looked around the table. "Everyone agreed?"

The others nodded. "I like it," Granger said. "Not only in memory of our old town, but for those that died too."

"Camp Benton it is. Tomorrow I'll go pick up some signs back in town and we'll put them up." Rollins stood up from the table, a pleased look on his face. "All right people, there's still a few hours of daylight left. Let's get back to work."

CHAPTER 20

Since burying Joe and Chrissie, Cody thought he was all done with disposing of bodies. He was wrong.

Their first task on arrival at Wasson Lodge was to check for any corpses inside. While there were signs that the seven bedrooms had been recently occupied, six of them were empty. In Room Three, however, four decomposing bodies lay together in a large double bed; a mother and father, and two young children that looked to have been around six and eight years old. To either side of the bed, the children's heads rested on their parent's chests, while the mother and father leaned in toward each other, their foreheads almost touching.

It was a gruesome, yet pitiful, sight, and none of the group relished the thought of having to remove them. After a short deliberation, Chris assigned Cody and Pete the job.

Chris had been unusually subdued during the negotiations with the Benton group. It was obvious he didn't enjoy the attention Walter was getting. Rollins and his deputy had been far more interested in Walter's skillset than in what Chris had to offer. His brashness and over-assertiveness hadn't done him any favors either.

As soon as they arrived at the camp, though, he reverted back to his normal self and immediately began organizing the work that needed to be done. To give him his due, he had been tireless, thriving on the challenge of setting the camp up. Chris wasn't somebody low on either ideas or confidence.

Of course, that had been when he put Cody and Pete on burial detail.

Cody's first instinct had been to refuse. He had a fair idea why Chris had assigned him the task. However, somebody had to do the job, and he didn't want it to appear like he wasn't prepared to be helpful.

It was summer. The bodies stank in a way that was almost unimaginable. They smelled like a piece of rotting meat that one flossed out of one's mouth, mixed with diarrhea and urine, multiplied by a factor of a hundred.

Luckily, Greta came to their aid. She gave them each gloves and surgical masks, onto which she added several drops of peppermint oil.

"That ought to help with the smell. It's an old nurse's trick," she told them.

Greta was a tall, athletic woman. Attractive, with shoulder-length dark hair, she had a no-nonsense way of speaking. *Bossy* was how Eddy described her. Cody simply put her manner down to her profession. Working in a hospital meant you spent a lot of time telling people what to do each day.

"Greta, you're not old!" Pete exclaimed. "You don't look more than thirty-five. That's ten years younger than me."

Greta stared at him frostily. "I'm thirty-four. I was talking about the trick, not me."

Cody and Pete wrapped each of the dead bodies up in a blanket and dragged them into the forest, where they doused them in gasoline and set them alight, thinking it a more hygienic way to dispose of them. Easier too.

While the bodies burned, they dug a shallow trench. Then, armed with spades, they scraped the charred remains into it. Chucking their gloves and masks into the grave afterward, they filled it in again, then made four small crosses and planted them along the trench.

Cody said a small prayer, the same one he'd said for Joe and Chrissie a few days ago, and the two trudged silently back to the camp.

"I'll say one thing for Chris, he's chosen a heck of a place," Pete said as they emerged from out of the forest and headed over to their trailers parked on the west side of the grounds. They were set apart from the rest of the group, who'd camped in a field overlooking a horseshoe bay at the back of the lodge. "Just look at the lake and all those mountains. Bound to be great hunting and fishing around here."

Cody nodded absently, thinking of something else. "Pete...I think Chris has it in for me," he said hesitatingly. "I knew he was going to put me on burial duty before he even opened his mouth."

"That so?" Pete said, looking across at him curiously.

Cody quickly went on to tell him what had occurred at the gas station earlier on. Listening carefully, Pete sighed once he finished. "So I'm on gravedigger duty with you through guilt by association, is that it? Okay, two points...you ready?"

"Sure, hit me."

"Point one. You're a good looking kid, same age as Emma. That makes you the competition. Point two. Chris is a competitive guy. Watch out."

Cody laughed. "Guess I better mind my step around here, that what you're saying?"

"Absolutely. Though lucky for you, maybe not for long. Walter wasn't too impressed with Chris down at the roadblock earlier. 'Man, that's one arrogant guy,' were his exact words. Who knows? Maybe the three of us will be moseying out of here sooner than you think."

"Really? Walter is planning on leaving already?" Pete's words alarmed Cody. Though he'd just met Emma, he felt a certain connection between them. He didn't want to have to leave the camp *that* quickly.

"He didn't say that exactly," Pete replied. "I'm just reading between the lines. We'll see, kid. It's early days."

CHAPTER 21

In downtown Knoxville, Mason Bonner sat in the living room of the luxurious condo he'd recently moved into, staring at the curved 50-inch UHD television on the wall. The TV wasn't on, but he stared at it anyway. Where else was he going to stare? Besides, the blank screen helped him think. Right now, he had plenty to think about too.

In the kitchen, Tania was preparing dinner. Without power, the fancy touch-control hob didn't work, so perched on top of it was a two-ring camping stove on which Mason could hear a pot coming to the boil.

"We eating pasta again?" he called out grumpily.

"Yeah, baby. Fettuccine with Alfredo sauce. That all right with you?"

"I guess. Though it'd be nice to have something different for a change."

Mason had only known Tania a week, and knew precious little about her life before the pandemic. One thing was for sure, though: she'd never spent much time in a kitchen. Stacked up on one side of the marble counter were jars of every conceivable pasta sauce imaginable, and Tania's idea of "changing things up" was to boil up pasta and throw a jar of exotic sauce over it. The previous night it had been puttanesca. The night before that, marinara. Today it was

127

Alfredo. Sure, it all sounded great, but right now Mason could kill a ribeye and fries. That wasn't happening anytime soon, though.

In fairness to Tania, his limited dietary regime wasn't just down to her. By now, all the fresh food had either disappeared or gone rotten in the supermarkets. Pasta served with tinned meat and bottled sauce was about the safest thing to eat.

Every day, food and water got that much harder to find. Dazed survivors who'd initially scavenged their meals one day at a time were now hoarding food or stocking up their vehicles and leaving town. With no supply trucks arriving in the city to replenish the supermarket shelves, things had reached a critical level.

It was why Mason controlled a gas station and three supermarkets across the city. Other street gangs had done similarly. It would keep his group in supply a while longer. Soon, though, like every other survivor, he would be forced to leave town, and with a crew of over twenty men and several women, he would be under pressure to keep them all fed.

Years ago, Mason had been a prison guard at Tennessee's state prison. Before being fired for displaying too many "overt sadistic tendencies", he'd witnessed enough to see how the gangs operated. If he failed to provide for them, his crew would soon fall apart.

One thing that favored a large gang such as his was, just like he could control a large section of the city, he could control a large patch of countryside. He just needed to figure out where. It was why he'd recently sent several scouts out of the city to find a suitable location.

There was a knock on the apartment door and Doney, Mason's chief bodyguard, a pale-faced, stocky man with quiffed black hair, poked his head in. Before vPox, the pair had worked together at a private security firm and had been the only two to survive.

In Doney's hand, he held a two-way radio. "Russ is downstairs. Says he needs to see you real urgent."

Mason raised an eyebrow. With other things pressing on his mind, he'd forgotten all about Russ, who he'd sent looking for Walter the previous day. "All right, bring him up," he said.

Over the radio, Doney instructed the downstairs guard to send Russ up. With so much gang activity in the city, Mason made sure he had adequate protection at the condo. You couldn't be too careful these days.

A few minutes later, Doney ushered Russ into the room. He was wearing a red and black motorcycle jacket and carried his helmet in one hand. He appeared hot and flustered, like he'd been riding for some time.

Mason stood up and came over to the door, staring Russ up and down. Small and ferret-like, he was unlikely to rise through the ranks of his organization. Still, with shiny, furtive eyes, he had a crafty intelligence that warranted attention.

"Well now," Mason said gruffly. "Wasn't sure I'd see you again. You got news for me?"

Russ nodded emphatically. "Sure do, Mason. I found Walter. It's better than that…he's still with Pete and the young guy who jumped us at the station, remember?"

Mason scowled. He wasn't the kind of guy who'd forget that afternoon in a hurry. It was why he'd sent Russ out to find them in the first place. "So where they at?"

Russ drew his breath. "They've joined a bigger group and left town. I spotted them on the I-40 this morning as they were leaving."

Mason frowned. This was yet another group who'd left the city. Pretty soon, his would be the only one left. "How big is this group?"

"Including Walter and the other two, there's twelve total. They drove out in trucks hauling trailers and went south to Lake Ocoee, down by the Georgia border."

"They going to stay there or head off again in the morning?"

"Can't say for sure, but it looked to me like they're planning on putting down roots," Russ replied. "They sure put a lot of work into persuading the guys at the roadblock to let them up to the lake. Once they—"

"Whoa, back up there. What damned roadblock you talking about?"

"There's already another group at the lake. They're at the YMCA camp," Russ explained. "They're well organized too. A few minutes after Walter arrived, a bunch of armed men showed up at the roadblock. From what I saw, they got a sheriff in charge of things. That's how it looked, anyway."

"And the sheriff let Walter and his people through?" Mason asked, a puzzled look on his face. In his book, letting a large group of strangers into your camp was an invitation for trouble.

Russ shook his head. "They didn't take the turn for the YMCA. The road continues on to a place called Wasson Lodge. I'm pretty sure that's where they went."

That made more sense. "What was the vibe between the two groups? Everyone get along?"

"Looked that way. The sheriff and Walter, along with another couple of guys, sure talked a long time."

"What's the distance between the YMCA and this lodge?"

Russ hesitated. "I'm not sure. I couldn't pass the roadblock to check it out. Not more than a couple of miles, I'm guessing."

"I see…"

Mason stood leaning against the wall, mulling over Russ's news. He'd never been to Lake Ocoee, but had heard about it. The area had been popular with hunters, and the forests were full of whitetails and wild boar. There were plenty of fish in the lakes and rivers too. Exactly the kind of place where a crew like his could set themselves up nicely, especially if somebody else put the hard work into fixing it up first. On top of that, if he could settle a score, all the better.

Russ stared at him, a sly grin on his face. "What you think, Mason? We go south and surprise the hell out of Walter?"

"Maybe. First I'm going to list down everything I need you to find out for me, then you're going to go back down and case the place out some more."

Russ gulped. "All right. When?"

"This evening." Mason pointed over to where Tania had just brought out a plate of steaming hot pasta and placed it on the table. "You hungry?"

Russ stared at the plate, his eyes practically eating it up. "I'm starving. I haven't eaten all day."

"Then get your ass over there. It's fettuccine with Alfredo sauce. Tania makes it real good." Mason turned to Doney, who'd stood waiting by the door all this time. "Radio down and get someone to fetch me a tin of salmon, barbecue chips, and a pack of cookies. If I eat one more pasta dish, I think I'll fucking puke."

CHAPTER 22

By the light of a kerosene lamp they'd hung on the wall, Ralph, Clete, and Maya sat at their usual spot in the Hilton bar. It was late evening. The two men drank Jack Daniels and Coke, while Maya was on the Laphroig.

"We're getting there," she said, taking a sip from her drink. "Day after tomorrow, we should be ready to leave."

Ralph nodded. "We got food, accommodation, and the wheels sorted. Tomorrow we pick up the hunting and camping gear. Right, Mr. Hillbilly?"

Clete grinned. "Damn straight."

That morning, Ralph and Maya had broached him about their plans to leave Atlanta, and whether he felt like heading out to Tennessee with them, seeing as he was from that way.

Clete's eyes had lit up like pinballs. "Why, I'd be happier than a tick on a bloodhound's balls!" he exclaimed. "Been telling Ralph we need to get out of the city ever since we got out of the joint. Pretty soon there'll be nothing left here but a bad smell. Can't wait to show you the place I'm thinking of taking you to. It's right on a beautiful lake."

Thirty minutes later, the three had left the hotel to start looking for everything they needed for their new life.

They began with transport. Clete insisted on American vehicles, and their first stop was a Ford dealership on the north side of the city. A short time later, they drove out in two brand new F-150 pickups, their motorcycles stored in the load beds. No way in hell was Ralph leaving his Harley behind.

They drove south on I-75 to Southern RV. Though it was on the far side of the city, it was the only trailer outlet Clete knew of. They picked up two nineteen-foot travel trailers. Hitching them up to their trucks, they spent the rest of the day in and out of supermarkets, snagging as much tinned and dry food as they could find, along with other provisions.

When they got back to the hotel, they unhitched the two trailers in the lot of the nearby Thrifty Car Rental, then drove their pickups into the Hilton underground parking area, where they unloaded the Harleys.

Maya had told Ralph that she rode motorcycles pretty well. She wasn't kidding. When she got out of the truck, she grabbed his keys, started the CVO, and roared out of the bay. Dropping the motorbike to its maximum lean angle, its foot peg scraping the concrete, she tore up the circular ramp. Outside the hotel entrance, as Ralph pulled up beside her on Clete's Dyna, she cut the engine and tossed him the keys.

He was liking this woman more and more.

He picked up his pack of Marlboros off the table, lighting one up. "Now Clete, you sure you're as good a hunter as you say you are, or were you just shooting your mouth off in the can?" People said all sorts of things in prison, where they had nothing better to do and no one to disprove them.

"Damn straight, I am!" Clete exclaimed. "My pa used to take me fishing and hunting since about as far back as I can remember. I can knock a squirrel out of a tree from seventy yards, and trap or hunt just about every critter that lives. Big or small, it don't matter to me."

Maya reached down and picked up her handbag from off the floor. Opening it, she took out a small notepad and pen, and placed them on the table. "How about we make a list of everything we need tomorrow?" she said. "This is your big chance to convince us you know what you're talking about. First off, where we going to find all our hunting gear?"

"There's a Dick's at Lennox Square," Ralph told her. "We should start there."

Clete shook his head. "I prefer Cabela's. There's one out at Acworth. It's a little far from here, but I know the store layout good. It'll save us time in the long run. We'll start with hunting, then move onto fishing and camping. We need good clothing too, for all seasons. This time of year it's hotter than two hamsters screwing in a wool sock. Come winter, it'll be colder than day-old penguin shit." He grinned at Maya. "If you pardon my French."

"Don't mind me, Mr. Hillbilly. I speak French pretty good too," she replied. "So…hunting?"

"We'll need rifles and shotguns. That's the kind of shit that goes fast, though. If there's nothing good left at Cabela's, we'll just have to bust open a gun store somewhere. Depending on the caliber weapons we find, I say we take all the ammo we can lay our hands on. Come to think of it, we should get ourselves some .22 rifles as well."

Ralph raised an eyebrow. "A hunting rifle, shotgun, *and* a .22? You sure you're not going a little overboard on this?"

"Nope. We need rifles to hunt deer and boar, a shotgun for birds, and a .22 for the squirrels." Clete looked at the two. "Ever seen a squirrel killed with a big ass .300 Winchester, 150-grain round?"

Ralph and Maya both shook their heads.

Clete chuckled. "Me neither. 'Cos there ain't nothing left. That's why you need a .22."

He went through fishing gear, followed by outdoor clothing, camping equipment, backpacks, range bags, and other necessary accessories. The more Clete added to the list,

135

including the simple items that made up his trapping kit: picture wire, bank line, and 16-penny nails, along with his explanation on exactly how they should be used, the more impressed Ralph became with his encyclopedia-like knowledge. While he was sure of his own skills in anything requiring a little muscle, his confidence in leaving the city grew with every item Maya added to the rapidly expanding list.

"Last thing…pack list," Clete said. "That's the list I make every time I head into the forest, the stuff that ticks me off if ever I forget to bring it with me. First thing that goes in is a compass. I've been hunting so long, I could get home blindfolded, but I take one all the same. Ain't nothing scarier than being lost in the woods, and it happens a lot easier that you think. Especially for you two. You got that, sweetheart?"

Maya nodded. At the top of a new page she'd written: PACK LIST. Below it, 1. COMPASS x 3.

"Next thing that goes in is a safety belt and a folding saw. That's for preparing a tree stand. My favorite way of catching deer. Boar too, for that matter. The safety belt allows you to stay in a tree for hours without falling out. Kinda important."

"And the folding saw?" Ralph asked.

"That's for cutting branches. You don't have that, forget ninety percent of the trees you want to select for a stand. Useful for making traps too, also firewood if you're camping out. Next in goes the binos and rangefinder. A rangefinder gives you the yardage of your prey. You'll need that for taking long range shots."

"Color me impressed," Ralph said. "Anything else?"

Clete scratched his head. "Can't forget the small stuff: gloves, matches, lighter, emergency blanket, and cordage. I think that's it, oh, and add deer scent…for luring the suckers in. We'll pick up a few all-season sprays, maybe some doe and buck urine for the fall."

"Buck urine? Fuck that," Ralph said, shaking his head. "That's where me and you part ways, Mr. Hillbilly."

Clete grinned. "Guess that'll just be my special sauce then. Well, that's about it. If I think of anything else, I'll let you know."

Maya placed the notebook and pen down on the table. "I have two more things we need to think about, that's gasoline and water." She stared at the two men. "We'll need to siphon as much gas as we can before leaving. Who knows where we can find it once we leave the city."

Ralph nodded. "We'll do the same with water. We got plenty today, but let's pick up some more. We got lots of room in the trailers to store it."

"Water is a real problem," Maya said. "It's going to run out fast. At some stage, we'll need to source it locally."

Clete looked at her thoughtfully. "There's giardia and all sorts of shit in river water. We'll need to pick up water purification tablets, filters too. 2 micron filters will get rid of any nasty ass bugs born in the USA. Seeing as everything is turning third world real fast, 1 micron would be even better."

Maya nodded. "Tomorrow I'll source the water purification tablets. A drugstore might have them. That ought to keep us going a while until we figure things out."

"Come to think of it, we should pick up a few boxes of powdered pool shock," Clete mused. "A pound of that will disinfect a hundred thousand gallons of water. It's got a long shelf life too. Add it to the list."

"Done," Maya said, chucking her notebook and pen down on the table again.

Clete stretched out his arms and yawned. "Think I'll hit the sack and leave you two lovebirds to it. Tomorrow we're going to be busier than a one-armed monkey with two peckers." Standing up, he grabbed his rifle from off the wall and headed out of the room.

"Looks like I'm going to be sporting a mullet and dungarees in no time," Ralph said dolefully once Clete had left.

"Stick to the biker look." Maya grinned. "That's how I like you."

The two talked some more. Maya sat with her back erect, her legs crossed, while Ralph slouched in his chair, a cigarette smoldering between his fingers and a soft buzz in his head from the Jack Daniels. He'd gotten comfortable at the Hilton. If it was in any way practical, he would have elected to stay in the city. Maya and Clete were right though. Soon, all that would be left was a bad smell. It was time to move on.

A short time later, in mid-conversation, Maya's voice trailed off. She stared in the direction of the bar entrance, her eyes widening.

"We got company," she said in a low voice. "Could be trouble."

Ralph swiveled in his seat to see two men armed with rifles step into the bar, spreading out as they crossed the room.

He leaped out of his chair and reached over to the wall to grab his Bushmaster.

"Pick that up and you're a dead man!" a harsh voice yelled out.

Ralph spun around. From behind the counter, another man stepped forward with a semi-automatic rifle raised to his shoulder. It was an AK-47, instantly recognizable from the distinct curved shape of its magazine. The man must have entered the bar ahead of his companions. Ralph cursed himself for not taking Clete's spot facing into the lobby after he'd left. Too much JD in his bloodstream had made him sloppy.

"The fuck you want?" he growled, his back to the wall.

"Start by reaching into your holster and take out your piece," the man told him. Short in stature, though barrel-chested and with muscular arms, he had dark, receding hair and several days' worth of stubble on his face. By now his companions had reached the table, their rifles pointing at Ralph.

Ralph didn't have much choice. He reached his hand across to his left hip and pulled out the cross-drawn Glock.

"Drop it on the floor and kick it over here."

Ralph bent down and laid the pistol on the carpet, kicking it away with the tip of his boot. Immediately, one of the men picked it up, then strode over and snatched his Bushmaster from off the wall.

The short guy took another couple of steps forward. "Well now," he said, staring at Ralph. "You're one handsome devil, ain't you? Who the hell cut your face up like that? Looks like somebody used it as a chopping board."

"A guy twice your size. He didn't survive to tell the tale though. While he was working on my face, I buried a shank in his liver."

The stranger smiled. "I can believe that. Though I'm guessing he didn't have two other men with the drop on you at the time, did he?"

"Nope. Just me and him." Ralph stared at the man. "What the hell you want? Plenty of room for everyone in town. Why don't you guys go across the street and check in at the Marriott?"

"Plenty of room, all right," the stranger agreed. "One thing there isn't plenty of, is talent." He turned his attention to Maya. "Darling, how long you known your boyfriend? Three days tops, I'm guessing."

"Two days," Maya replied coolly. "We met right here in this bar."

The man grinned. "So it's not like you two are in love."

Maya shrugged. "Not much room for love in these times. I'm a practical girl, just looking for someone to take care of me, that's all." She glanced at Ralph, who stared back at her stony-eyed.

The stranger spread his arms open. "Why honey, I'd be happy to take care of you," he said with a wolfish grin. "I'm not as big as your friend here, but I got my own crew. Eight in total. That counts for a lot more these days." He turned to his two companions. "What did I tell you? Soon as I saw this girl ride her Harley up here this evening, I said to myself, that's my kind of woman."

"Careful, Marty, I don't trust her," one of the men growled. "Look at her eyes jumping all over the place. She's just looking for an angle to get out of this."

"Well, there ain't no angle," Marty replied flatly, "And who said anything about trusting her? I just plan on having some fun, that's all." He waved his pistol at Maya. "All right, darling. Up you get. I'm taking you back to my side of town. Don't worry, you'll still be living in style. It's another five star hotel."

Maya hesitated. "All right, I won't cause you any problems. So long as you don't hurt Ralph. There's no need for that."

Marty shook his head. "It's touching to see such loyalty, but see, your boyfriend looks the sort who holds a grudge. Can't risk that." He swiveled the AK toward Ralph, still standing by the wall. "Time to say bye-bye Ralph, hello Marty."

"Wait!" Maya called out. "At least let me say goodbye properly." Before Marty could stop her, she jumped up out of her seat and walked around the table to Ralph. With her back to the three strangers, she spread out her arms to hug him. "I'm sorry, but what can I do? It's the times we live in."

Ralph shrugged. "I guess so."

Obscuring Marty's view, Maya stepped in closer and slowly closed her eyes. Ralph caught a brief whiff of Shalimar perfume as he whipped his P225 from the rig behind his back. Lifting it over her shoulder, he aimed and squeezed the trigger.

A single shot rang out, and a 115-grain jacketed hollow point blew a hole in Marty's chest. Mushrooming on impact, it went in like a penny and out the far side like a pizza, busting through a chunk of his aorta in the process. With a short grunt, he dropped to the floor.

His two companions desperately raised their rifles to their shoulders. Ralph's P225 was far the quicker to aim, and several more shots rang out around the bar in rapid succession.

The man standing closest to Ralph went down first. Double-tapped in the chest, he toppled face first to the ground. A second later, his companion staggered to one side, then fell over onto his back. Ralph finished him off, then lowered his weapon.

Maya turned around to see the three men on the floor without so much as a single twitch between them. Dead as doornails. She drew her breath and whistled. "You've done that before, haven't you?"

"I might have had a little practice," Ralph admitted. He stared down at the P225 in his grip. "Not bad for a *just in case* gun."

"I'll say."

There was the sound of someone running through the lobby. A moment later, Clete burst into the room, his Colt M4 raised to his shoulder. He strode over to them, stopping when he saw the three bodies on the floor.

"Aw, I missed all the action, didn't I?"

"Yep," Ralph grunted, slotting the Sig into the waistband holster behind his back. He walked over to one of the slain men and retrieved his Bushmaster and Glock. "Thanks for showing up, though. It's the thought that counts."

Clete stooped over Marty and picked up the dead man's rifle. He gazed down the barrel appreciatively. "Now this here AK can join our hunting collection," he said. "At two hundred yards, a 7.62 round is real sweet for taking down a wild pig. Trust me on that."

Ralph grinned. "You crazy hillbilly. Now you really are going overboard with the guns."

CHAPTER 23

The following morning, the Knoxville group convened in the lodge's huge living room for their first meeting. Earlier, Chris had washed and shaved down at the lakeside. He'd combed his hair, and wore a white Ralph Lauren polo shirt, a pair of crisply pressed khaki shorts, and looked very much the high-flying executive on a team-building weekend – with him as team leader, of course.

"Good morning, people," he said, coffee in hand, flashing an energetic smile around the room. "I hope everyone got a good night's sleep, because we've got another busy day ahead of us."

A murmur of yeses went around the room.

"All right. Seeing as yesterday was our first day, we went about getting stuff done without too much fuss. Today I'm going to assign formal roles for everyone here at the camp. It's important we build a proper structure. Right now, there're twelve of us in total. That number is only going to grow, so—"

"Chris, before you assign roles, I have a question," Walter cut in. "You say you're assigning everyone their roles. Shouldn't that decision, along with all other decisions, be decided by an elected council, rather than just *you*? Makes for a fairer system, in my opinion."

An annoyed frown came over Chris's face. "Maybe you haven't figured it out yet, Walter, but democracy is dead. This is a survival situation we got here. We're going to face tough challenges. Challenges that may threaten our very existence. The group needs a leader who can make the right decisions in those situations, not some squabbling council."

Walter raised an eyebrow. "So you've proclaimed yourself king, that it?"

"Call it what you will," Chris said, staring at him coldly. "This is my group. I assessed and handpicked every person in this room individually. Except for you three. It's why you're still only provisional members so far. I've yet to decide if you're a good fit or not."

"Likewise," Walter replied coolly. "All right, go ahead. Sorry for the interruption."

Shooting him a final look, Chris continued speaking. "We'll start off with security arrangements. Last night, I met with Sheriff Rollins and keyed in one of our radios to the Benton group channel. That way we can be kept up to date with outside events. I've given him a list of all our names, and he's going to instruct those on duty at the roadblock not to allow anyone else up to the lodge without my specific permission."

He stared down at his notes. "I'm designating Eddy as our chief of security. He's had extensive weapons training and is a sharpshooter with both handguns and rifles. As such, he'll be in charge of managing our perimeter defenses, coordinating with the Benton group on security matters, and making sure everyone here is fully trained in handling guns. I know some of you are a little uncomfortable with that, but we've got a great setup here, we need to protect it. Make no mistake about it, at some stage we're going to need to defend this settlement."

"Really?" Liz asked nervously from over the far side of the room. A short, stocky woman with gray hair who, according to Eddy, was a botanist. Cody guessed Chris intended putting her in charge of growing food at the camp.

"There are so few survivors, and so much land for everyone. Why would anyone want to take over our camp when they can set up their own?"

"Because gangs like to rob and steal. They'd prefer to occupy an existing camp rather than build one for themselves." Chris shrugged. "Just the way it is."

Walter nodded. "Remember, not all gangs will be made up of *bad* people. Pretty soon, regular folk will become a problem too. Once food and water runs out in the cities, they'll head to places like this. They'll be aggressive. Hunger does that to a person. If they see us as a soft target, they'll come right in and take whatever they—"

"That's right," Eddy interrupted, anxious to get a word in. "First thing we're going to do is prepare tripwire around the lodge, so we can hear if anyone approaches. Particularly at night, when we're most vulnerable. I plan on building a perimeter fence too, topped with razor wire. That'll stop anyone from rushing at us, catching us unprepared."

"Absolutely," Chris agreed. "The better prepared we are, the better chance people will move on and look for a softer target." He leaned forward in his chair, staring around the group eagerly. "We got a real chance to build something good here. Something of value. Sure, none of us are preppers, we're learning this as we go along, but I plan on us thriving here. That means we need to be sure to hold onto this place. Agreed?"

A murmur of assent went around the room. While at times Chris's manner was abrasive, capable of rubbing people up the wrong way, at the same time, he had an abundance of energy, a ferocious will that was something to behold. His words rang true around the room. Even Mark and James, who both appeared rather introverted from what Cody had observed so far, looked enthused. Sitting together, the two leaned forward in their chairs, listening attentively.

"Good. Next item…Greta, I see you've converted the children's den into a mini hospital ward, that right?"

Greta nodded. "Correct. I've stocked it with all my medical equipment and supplies. For the moment, it's only got two beds. Lord forbid, if we were ever to have several people injured at any one time, it can easily handle a few more." She glanced around the room. "For those of you that aren't aware, I'm a trained ER nurse and worked at the Parkwest Emergency Care Center for seven years. While I'm not a doctor, I can deal with everyday problems. I can stitch wounds, set broken limbs, and diagnose most ailments." She smiled. "Other than the X-Ray machine, I've pretty much brought the entire stock of Parkwest ER with me."

"How about gunshot injuries?" Tim asked. "You ever treat them?"

Greta nodded grimly. "Plenty. Right now, though, our main concern is potable water. Once our bottled supply runs out, waterborne disease is a real risk. We have enough to last us about another week. After that, we'll need to take it from a nearby water source. It'll need to be boiled, and I've brought plenty of bleach too. We'll use that to make double-sure we kill all disease organisms."

Pete pointed out the window to the lake. "Our nearest water source is fifty feet away. Are you planning on hauling water from there?"

Greta hesitated a moment. "I'm not an expert, but my understanding is that it's best to get our supply from moving water. I'm going to visit Camp Ocoee today. I'll find out what they're doing there, then make a decision."

"Camp Benton," Chris corrected her. "That's what they're calling it."

"Greta," Walter cut in, "I've brought the parts to build a simple water purification system. It's just a couple of five gallon buckets and a ceramic filter, but it'll do the job. Either lake or river water will do just fine."

"Excellent," Greta replied, looking at Walter approvingly. "Given we're such a large group, how long do you expect the filter to last?"

"It'll give us fifteen gallons a day for the next twelve months, so we're good for a while." Walter smiled. "Just so happens, I brought a couple of extra filters with me too."

"Very good," Chris said, looking pleased. He consulted his notes again. "All right, we've brought plenty of dry foods with us, specifically rice, wheat, corn, and pasta. Enough to last several months. There are plenty of farms in the area. In fact, there's one less than a mile away. It's close to the Baptist church, if I remember correctly. Liz is going to go down there today. She'll take a look and see what sort of vegetables we can start growing."

"Right," Liz said. "I'll also do a general search of the area and round up whatever farm animals have survived. I saw cows in a field on our way up here yesterday. I'm hoping to find pigs and chickens too. In this weather though, without water, unless they were let out of their pens and coops, they may all be dead. Still, you never know." She paused a moment. "Another thing. We need to be careful checking these places out. There may be survivors at them. Some may not be too keen on talking to us either."

"Why not?" Chris asked, frowning.

"Before the Internet went down, there was a rumor going around that those of us with immunity to vPox could be carriers. People who've had no contact with the disease and have isolated themselves at remote locations might not want to risk talking to us. They may even shoot at us."

There was silence around the room while the group considered the implications of what Liz just said. Nobody had thought of that before.

"As for agriculture, it looks like they grew mainly soybeans around here," she continued. "We'll need to get a lot more diverse than that. The good news is, I raided several gardening stores before we left Knoxville. I'm confident we'll get something going soon."

"That reminds me," Walter said. "Back in Ocoee yesterday, we passed a farm store. We need to get back there soon and pick up supplies. It should have plenty of useful stuff."

"Like what?" Chris asked.

"Rolls of barbed wire and T-Posts for defense. Water storage tanks, and galvanized tubs for washing clothes. Not to mention all that wheat and corn we can grind into flour and cornmeal."

Chris rubbed his hands together. "Excellent," he said, his eyes shining. "All right, regarding protein, we got plenty of canned beef, ham, and tuna, though I'd prefer to hold onto as much of it as possible for emergencies. Good thing is, the lake is full of bass and catfish, there's trout streams nearby, and whitetail and feral pigs in the forest." He gazed around the room. "Who among us other than Eddy knows how to hunt?"

Cody shot his hand up like an eager schoolchild. "I'm a good hunter. My dad taught me to hunt in the Chattahoochee forest south of here."

Chris smiled at him, though his eyes didn't show a lot of enthusiasm. "Great. When was the last time you hunted?"

Cody hesitated. "It was a while back. Maybe eight years ago."

Chris frowned. "You could only have been twelve or thirteen at the time."

"I was fourteen. Don't worry, I have a real good eye," Cody assured him.

"The kid can shoot," Pete chimed in. "He killed two people in a moving vehicle back in Knoxville. Put down two more on the gas station forecourt."

"Tim, how about you?" Chris said, turning away. "You told me you used to hunt."

"When I was younger," Tim said hesitantly. "I've put on some weight since then. I'm not so mobile these days."

Chris looked at him sharply. "Spending time in the forest will get the weight off you fast. I'm going to nominate you alongside Eddy."

Cody's face fell. While he could always hunt in his spare time, he'd really wanted this role. He was certain that Chris envisaged a less exciting job for him though, something with a little less allure. Perhaps he'd already been earmarked to build latrines? Gravedigger, shit shoveler, that would be sure to put Emma off the scent. Quite literally.

Greta caught his crestfallen look. "Chris, give Cody a shot at it," she said sternly. "Doesn't do any harm. He's young and athletic. Personally, my money is on him coming home with the meat ahead of Tim. No offense, Tim."

"None taken," Tim said, looking relieved. "I say we give the kid a chance too. Once I lose a couple of pounds, I'll give him a run for his money," he added with a chuckle.

"All right, we'll give him a tryout," Chris said reluctantly. "Eddy, how about you take Cody out into the forest later? See how he gets on. This is a job with a lot of responsibility. If he's not up to it, I need to know right away."

Eddy looked over at Cody, a sour look on his face. "I'll check him out good. Don't worry."

While Chris continued to delegate positions to the remaining members of the group, Cody began mentally planning for the hunt. Something told him he'd have to really prove himself if he was going to keep this job.

CHAPTER 24

Shoulder to shoulder, Sheriff Rollins strode alongside Ned Granger as the two men toured the defenses in progress at Camp Benton. Since the crack of dawn, Granger had been working tirelessly on building its perimeter, constructing guard posts, sniper's hides, and foxholes, and devising the strategies to be employed if they came under attack.

"By tomorrow, the initial phase will be complete, with everyone drilled on what to do," he told Rollins confidently. "They'll know where to go, what avenues of attack they should defend and, if need be, the next line of defense they should retreat to. Understanding your role, maintaining discipline, and proper weapons training will be what keeps this property defended."

"Along with some damned fine planning," Rollins said, slapping him on the shoulder. "How is Mary doing?"

While Granger organized the camp's defenses, Mary Sadowski had been in charge of firearms practice at an improvised shooting range she'd set up.

"She's doing great. The perfect person for the job," Granger replied. "She's practical, a natural leader, and a damned good shot too."

Strolling along the camp's north shore, the two men reached the point where the long, narrow inlet Rollins had marked on the map the previous day tapered to an end.

"Let's walk the perimeter," Granger said. "Soon we'll have four dug-in positions and an observation post that we've named Papa One through Five. They'll stretch from here across to the south bay. Papa One is already built. Come on, I'll show you."

Rollins followed Granger into the forest, weaving in and out through the trees. Ten yards in from the lake shore, they reached a spot where, between two trees, a T-shaped trench had been built, its sides shored up with planks so that the walls didn't cave in. The stem of the T was fifteen feet long. At the top, several burlap sandbags stacked two-high had been placed. In the trench stood a man named Jim Wharton, an AR-15 resting across the top of the sandbag.

"Howdy, Sheriff," he greeted Rollins cheerfully as the two men approached.

"Afternoon, Jim," Rollins replied.

Slightly overweight, with a round face and wispy blond hair, Wharton had been an agricultural sales man back in Benton. Rollins hadn't known him well, only enough to nod to.

Granger jumped down into the trench and indicated that Rollins jump in after him.

"Jim's our top shooter," Granger told him. "As you can see, there's plenty of room for more men to defend this position if necessary." He pointed behind him along the T's stem. "Here's the escape route if they need to retreat." He grinned at Rollins. "In case you're wondering how come we built it so fast, we brought in a mini excavator from Benton this morning. By tomorrow, we should have all four positions built, two on either side of the driveway."

Rollins stared out over the sandbags and into the forest. "How far back has the tripwire been laid?"

"Thirty yards," Granger replied. "Close enough to hear anyone, far enough to give the sentry time to radio in for help."

Granger led Rollins farther into the woods, skirting around Papa Two where the mechanical digger was noisily scooping out earth. They emerged from the forest and onto the camp driveway.

"This stretch of road gives us a good view both ways," Granger explained. "If a force somehow managed to sneak past our checkpoints and guard posts, we wouldn't want them to just march up the driveway to the camp, would we? John, where would you place an observational post around here?"

Rollins took a good look around. To either side of the road, he saw no sign of anything manmade. There were no trenches or sandbags in sight. He tilted his head. Shading his eyes from the sun, he gazed up into the trees. On his second scan, he spotted a large tree twenty feet away where several wooden planks had been nailed across two sturdy branches. Sitting with his back against the trunk was a figure in dark green camos.

Rollins pointed up at him. "I'd place Papa Three right about there."

Granger grinned. "Well spotted. And we've got a nasty surprise for anyone who makes it this far." He pointed farther up the driveway, toward the camp. "There's sandbag positions lined along the side of the road. By the time anyone makes it to here, they'll be in the middle of a kill zone." He grabbed Rollins's shoulder. "Come on, I've one more thing to show you."

The two men crossed the driveway and walked through the forest, passing where posts Papa Four and Five would soon be constructed, then headed toward the south bay. Walking along the peninsula's jagged shoreline, they reached the southernmost point where, overlooking the lake, was a family cabin.

"The YMCA named this cabin 'Apache'," Granger said as they reached it. "I've renamed it the South Beach Post. Better to have a visual name for it. There's a similar position at the northern tip as well – the North Beach Post. While I expect any attack will most likely come from land, we need lookouts on the lake both north and south. We can't afford to get caught off guard."

Due south of the cabin was a clear view of the Baker Creek Inlet, its crystalline blue waters sparkling in the morning sun. It was a large expanse, more a bay than an inlet. At the very end, and out of sight, was where Route 302 passed by.

Walking around to the front of the cabin, Granger pointed up at the porch roof. Staring out at the lake, a man sat on a cushion, a pair of binoculars dangling on his chest. Rollins recognized the man, though wasn't personally acquainted with him. Even in a small town such as Benton, he hadn't come to know absolutely everyone.

"Sherriff, this is Bob Harper." Granger introduced the man. "How you doing, Bob?"

"Everything's good, Ned. Nothing to report."

Granger checked his watch. "Not long to go. Another forty minutes and your shift will be over."

Harper grinned. "I'll be heading straight to the canteen. I'm famished."

Rollins made a quick calculation. With four men currently down at the two Cookson roadblocks, five soon to be stationed along the forest perimeter, along with another two guarding the lake shore, it made for a grueling schedule for thirty-two adults. He voiced his concern to Granger.

Granger nodded. "Once the Knoxville group settles in, I propose we dismantle both Cookson roadblocks and build a proper barrier on the driveway where Papa Three is. We won't need the OP anymore, so it'll free up three persons."

Rollins looked at him doubtfully. "That's going to expose Chris and his group. There's only eight of them."

Granger shrugged. "It's their property now. It's up to them to defend it."

"Still, if they get overrun, it exposes us too," Rollins insisted. "Let's think about that some more."

They headed back toward the camp. "I think we're good to stave off any daytime raid," Granger said as the two strolled along the lake shore. "My main worry is a nighttime attack. It's harder to defend in the dark. People just waking up are more likely to panic, especially those who've never come under fire before."

"Keep drilling them," Rollins replied. "Rouse them at four a.m. for the next few days until they get used to it."

"Don't worry, Mary and I intend doing that. Once we get the primary defenses finished, I plan on building a fallback position where we can regroup if the perimeter gets overrun. And I've got a surprise up our sleeves for anyone sneaking in here during the dead of night too."

"What exactly?" Rollins asked, curious.

"When we get back, I'll show you." Granger grinned. "Something I picked up in Cleveland yesterday."

CHAPTER 25

As soon as the meeting ended, Cody went back to his trailer and fixed himself a second breakfast, consisting of cereal soaked in OJ, dry salami, and a sugary black instant coffee. After he ate, he spent the next twenty minutes getting ready for the hunt. Good preparation was everything, his father used to tell him. He tingled with excitement, a little nervous too. Chris had made it plain that this hunting expedition was to be a test. He would only get one shot (quite literally, perhaps) at applying for the role as hunter in the group.

He was outside unhitching his trailer when Eddy showed up. They quickly slung their gear into the back of Cody's truck and drove out of the camp. Above them, a bright yellow sun beat down from the cloudless blue skies, and Cody turned the air con onto full blast.

At the end of the driveway, he steered left and quickly arrived at the South Cookson roadblock. After radioing their camp, the two Benton guards waved them through and they wound their way east along Lake Ocoee's southern shore. The previous evening, Sheriff Rollins had given Chris several copies of a detailed U.S. Forest Service map of the area. Cody was grateful to have one. Surrounding them was a spider's web of roads, trails and forestry tracks that required careful navigation.

A mile out of camp, the road swung north. After another mile, they came to a crossroads, where they turned onto Baker Creek Road and headed east in the direction of an area known as Harris Branch. From the map, they could see it was comprised of a small clearing in the middle of the forest. Far away from human habitation, both men agreed it would be a good place to look for game. A 12-point buck was on Cody's mind, though he would settle for a pig. Anything but return to camp with *nada*.

Fifteen minutes later, they reached the clearing. Cody drove under the shade of a large oak tree and pulled up. Once the two had gotten out, he locked up the Tacoma.

Though only ten a.m. he immediately began to sweat. Mid-June, the temperature had been increasing these past few days, and insects buzzed around his face. He grabbed his day pack and took out the mosquito repellent. After spraying his arms, face and neck, he handed it to Eddy.

As well as picking out a hunting rifle and fishing gear at Dick's that day, Cody had also selected plenty of outdoor clothing, the best that money could buy. Today he wore a baseball cap, nylon hiking pants, a short sleeve omni-wick shirt, thick socks, and a pair of good waterproof boots.

Inside his pack were a few snack bars, beef jerky, spare water, spare ammo, spare socks, a hatchet, a length of rope, a rolled-up heavy duty plastic bag, and a first aid kit. Strapped to either side of his belt were his Kimber and his fixed blade hunting knife. In the side pocket of his pants he carried a compass.

Eddy was similarly dressed, other than he wore shorts rather than long pants. Cody thought it a poor choice. In the forest, his legs would get badly scraped.

Eddy nodded at him curtly. "Let's go."

Briefly checking the map, the two headed south in the direction of the Conasauga River, five miles south of their position, starting down a forest track that wound its way along the side of a narrow valley.

"We'll need to keep our eyes on the ground as well as watch out for game," Cody said. "Plenty of copperheads and rattlesnakes around here."

Eddy gave him a look. "I know, kid. I know."

Slung over Cody's shoulder was a Remington Sendero SFII. Like all good hunting rifles, it was bolt-action, chambered for a .300 Magnum round. With its 26-inch barrel for long range accuracy, and the scope on, it weighed over ten pounds. Heavier than most, it was based on the older 700 model his father used to own. It was the reason he'd chosen it.

Eddy had brought a .308 caliber Sakko Finlight. It was a lighter gun, and in his opinion, a better rifle than the Remington. They would soon see.

Emerging out of thick forest, the trail took them through open woodland. They passed a creek, hiked up and down several hills, all the time the sun getting stronger.

"Damn, it's hotter than hell," Eddy griped after about twenty minutes, wiping his face.

"How about we get off the trail and into the forest?" Cody suggested. "It'll be cooler, and that's where we'll find the deer." Eddy had the map and had been giving the directions until now. Cody had been patiently waiting for him to suggest this.

Eddy shrugged. "All right."

Once off the track, the going got tougher as they made their way through ferns and briars. Cody couldn't help but smile to think how Eddy's legs were faring, and every so often, he let out a loud curse. Under the thick forest canopy, it was far cooler, though.

After a while, they crossed another creek and entered into a large clear cut.

"This is a good spot for deer," Cody said.

"Why do you say that?"

"We've got steep terrain to either side of an open clearing. It's a typical funnel for deer to pass through." Cody pointed out a tree at the far end of the clearing. "That's white oak. During fall, this is where they'll come to eat."

"Yeah, but it's not fall," Eddy objected.

"True, but unless there's a good reason, they won't move too far away from it."

Farther ahead was a sapling tree. Cody walked over to it and stopped. Eddy followed him over.

"Deer rub," Cody said, pointing at the base where the bark had been removed. "Too early in the year to have been made recently though. See how there's no fresh markings? Still, we're in a travel corridor, that's for sure."

"Dammit, kid. You're good," Eddy said grudgingly.

Cody grinned. Perhaps Eddy was a good marksman at the range, but by now he'd have figured out he didn't know a damn thing about hunting, and Cody felt confident in taking the lead. "Next time, we'll set up a stand somewhere along the corridor, but that's a waiting game and best done on your own. For now, let's see if we get lucky."

Farther ahead, they came across a tiny forest trail that took them up a steep sloped spur and into the hills. Cresting the ridge, they gazed down into a lightly forested valley. About to continue on, Cody raised a hand to Eddy's chest.

"Wait," he whispered, pointing down at a small stand of pines.

He lifted his rifle and peered through the scope. Eddy did likewise. Two hundred yards away, in a patch of briars and hawthorn, a buck grazed. He looked about two hundred and fifty pounds, about the average weight of a mature whitetail. The huge antlers atop his head looked grossly out of proportion to the rest of his body.

The buck was facing head-on, but hadn't spotted the pair yet. With them being downwind of him, he hadn't picked up their scent.

"That's a hell of a rack," Eddy whispered excitedly. Both had dropped to one knee, staring at the buck through their scopes. "What do you think? Worth taking a pop?"

"Not yet," Cody whispered back. "Too difficult a shot. Best to wait until he turns broadside."

"All right. When he turns, I'm taking the first shot."

Eddy's blood was up. He wanted to claim the kill, even though Cody had been the one to spot the buck. If he missed, the whitetail would wheel away, making Cody's shot far harder.

A few moments later, the buck slowly turned.

"Now," Cody whispered.

Eddy took a moment to steady his aim, then fired. There was a sharp crack. Through his scope, Cody saw the deer raise its head in alarm. Eddy had missed.

As the buck took a step, quartering away, Cody fired. The shot hit the buck just behind the shoulder, right on the money, where the heart and lungs were. It staggered, then dropped to its knees and keeled over.

"Dammit, kid! That's a hell of a shot!" Eddy exclaimed, unable to help himself.

Cody lowered his rifle and grinned. "Thanks." He stood up. "Come on, our work's not done yet. Here comes the messy part."

Hiking down the valley slope, they approached the buck from the side away from its legs, just like Cody's father had taught him. He withdrew his Kimber. A downed animal was not necessarily a dead animal, and thrashing legs could cause serious injury, especially a big one like this. Checking its chest movement, Cody saw that it wasn't breathing. He examined its eyes and noted they were glazed.

"It's dead," he said.

He holstered the Kimber, lay down his pack and rifle on the ground, turning the deer over onto its back.

He took out his hunting knife. "Okay, here goes." Locating the sternum, he made an incision through the hide and abdominal wall.

"Shouldn't we slit his throat and bleed him out first?" Eddy asked.

"No need. A normal field dressing is going to do that anyway."

Careful not to cut any of the buck's internal organs, he slit the animal's belly open and removed its bladder and urinary tract.

Engrossed, Eddy watched Cody roll the carcass onto its side and allow its entrails to roll out. "You're a real killer. No doubt about it," he marveled.

"My dad taught me well," Cody replied, cutting away to fully free the entrails. "Even if I was only fourteen years old."

He cut the diaphragm away from the ribcage, rolled the buck over again, and took out the heart and lungs.

Holding up the heart, he pointed to his pack. "Fetch out the plastic bag. We'll keep the heart and liver."

Eddy screwed up his face. "Who the hell is going to eat that?"

"Me, for one," Cody replied. "You know what parts of the body a wild animal eats first? The heart, liver, and kidneys. They're the most nutritious parts."

"I'll stick to a nice venison steak," Eddy replied, unconvinced.

After draining the body cavity of blood, they were ready to go. What remained of the buck was still a heavy weight to carry, however. Cody took out his hatchet and went about cutting down a sturdy branch from a nearby tree. Delimbing it, the two bound the buck's legs at both ends with twine, then slung the pole through it.

Lifting the pole up by either end, they raised it over their shoulders and began the march back to the pickup.

"So, do I pass the test?" Cody asked as they trudged back up the hill.

"Yeah, kid. You passed," Eddy replied, breathing heavily. "You're a natural born killer. Ain't no point denying it."

Cody smiled. He looked forward to seeing the look on Chris's face at the following morning's meeting.

CHAPTER 26

Jonah and Colleen spent the morning planning everything they needed for their upcoming journey. They intended leaving Orlando the following day. The previous evening, they had talked to Klaus and the American woman, Susan, inviting them to come with them. Both had politely declined.

Susan was from Baltimore and anxious to return and look for any surviving family members. Klaus had offered to accompany her, and the two had departed at dawn that morning. Secretly, Jonah was relieved to hear the news and suspected Colleen felt the same. The couple would fare better on their own.

While Jonah knew everything he needed off the top of his head, Colleen prepared a comprehensive list. Some of it she scribbled down from memory, then spent another hour scanning through her Kindle and adding additional items, tut-tutting when she forgot something she felt she ought to have remembered, such as a blood-clotting agent, which she added to the first aid section.

"It stems the blood flow of serious injuries," she explained to Jonah, sitting beside her on the bed. "Like gunshot wounds, for instance."

With their newly-acquired Glock 21s strapped in holsters by their waists, and their Armalite M-15s slung over their shoulders (which Bill O'Shea had assured Jonah was a fine rifle), the two left the hotel.

Their first stop was the North Face outlet on West Oak Ridge Road. Jonah had stumbled across it the previous day when he'd taken the wrong exit coming back from the gun shop with Klaus. Inside the store, they picked out matching dark-green backpacks.

Initially, Jonah chose one in "Papaya Orange" for Colleen. "Kinda perky," he said when he showed it to her. "You'll look hot on the trail wearing this."

"No," Colleen argued. "People will spot it a mile away. I don't think that's what we want."

Jonah immediately took her point. While he mightn't have read any post-apocalyptic books, he'd seen *Deliverance* many times. The thought of Colleen and him being chased through the forest or forced to squeal like a pig didn't appeal to him very much.

They selected a couple of sleeping bags, a tent, a tarp, and a ground pad. Also hiking boots, rain gear, fleece jackets, shorts, waterproof pants, hats, caps, and gloves.

After that they drove to the Florida Mall, a huge mall ten minutes farther south. Cruising the building, they saw that someone had already busted open the entrance leading into the food court. Pistols in hand, they headed inside and wandered around the complex until they found a CVS.

Jonah pried open the pharmacy's glass door with a goose-necked jimmy he'd found in a utility room back at the hotel that morning. Inside, he took another gander at the first aid list:

Antibiotics, Antibacterial Cream, Anti-Diarrheal tablets

Tourniquet, Gauzes, Trauma Pad, Bandages, Burn salve, Splints & Suture Kit

Band Aids, Butterfly strips, latex gloves, medical tape & pain killers

Hydrogen Peroxide, Blood Clotting Agent & Super Glue

"Super glue…on a first aid list?" Jonah said, raising an eyebrow. Colleen had added another item since he last looked.

"To button up that big mouth of yours," she replied with a grin. "Actually, it's perfect for wound closure. Keep an eye out for SurgiSeal or Dermabond. They're the two best known brands."

Twenty minutes later, they'd found everything they needed except for the suturing kit. "Let's keep an eye out for a veterinary hospital or clinic on our way back," Colleen commented. "They ought to have them."

They moved on. In the northwest section of the mall, they came across a Dick's Sporting Goods outlet. To their delight, it had a hunting department, where they threw a bunch more stuff into the two canvas bags they'd picked up earlier: Leatherman multipurpose knives, buck knives with a seven-inch blade (for cutting game), a pair of Steiner Tactical 10x binoculars (for spotting game – and the bad guys), a pair of Sightmark Ghost Hunter 2x night vision binoculars (for spotting the bad guys in the dark).

They also picked up equipment to purify water: Lifestraws, Sawyers filters, and a Katadyn pump filter. Last but not least, several cans of pepper spray and a machete. The pepper spray was in case of a bear attack, Colleen explained.

Thirty minutes later, the two hauled their goodies back through the mall and out the south side entrance, where they'd parked the Taurus in front of the food court.

"That's us set for tomorrow," Colleen said, a satisfied look on her face as the two packed everything into the car.

Jonah grinned. "I haven't seen you this excited since Leicester won the Prem," he said, referring to a few years back when Leicester City had won the English Premiership. At the start of the season, the odds of them winning had been five thousand to one. In the closing few games, half of Europe, including Jonah and Colleen, had willed them on.

"Jonah, I'm not happy with any of this," Colleen reprimanded him. Relenting a little, she added, "We're dealing with things well, but we're still at a critical stage of our survival. Let's see where we are in a week's time."

They made one more stop on the way back to the hotel. One Jonah insisted on. Pulling up outside a liquor store, from his back pocket he pulled out his own list:

Jack Daniels x6 btls
Budweiser x48 tins
White Wine x1 btl (for Colleen)

Opening the driver door, he grabbed the jimmy. "Right love, just getting a bit of gargle for the trip. You know, to get me through this critical stage of our survival. I'll be back in a jiffy."

Colleen rolled her eyes and sighed. "Jonah Murphy, you're lucky I love you very much."

***

Returning to the Sun Ray, the couple wearily hauled their canvas bags up the emergency stairs. It had been another scorching day, and the smell in the hotel had gotten worse.

"*Jaysus*, that stink is bleedin' woeful," Jonah said, pinching his nose as they emerged from the stairwell onto the second floor. "I tell yeh, I won't be sorry to see the back of this kip."

Once inside their room, Jonah immediately dropped his gear and rushed into the bathroom, where he grabbed a towel, then his aftershave from off the shelf. Rolling up the towel, he brought it into the bedroom and planted it across the foot of the hall door.

He unscrewed the bottle of aftershave and poured it across the towel. "That'll get rid of the smell," he said. "You know, I could do with a bit of that meself." Splashing the remaining drops of aftershave onto his fingers, he daubed it on both sides of his face, then chucked the bottle on the floor.

Colleen wrinkled her nose at the pungent smell wafting toward her. "I'm not sure whether you've made things better or worse," she said, frowning. "Did you really need to pour it all on?"

Jonah shrugged. "I'll take the smell of Old Spice over Old Pox any day of the week. Come on, let's start packing so we're ready to go first thing in the morning."

He opened the canvas bags and began pulling out the contents, placing them on the bed. "I'll say one thing about the a*pox*alypse," he said with a grin. "It's great the way yeh can grab whatever yeh want in the stores, no matter what the price tag says. If you include the shooters, we must have over ten grand's worth of gear here."

"Jonah, don't call it the a*pox*alypse!" Colleen said in an exasperated tone. "This isn't a joke. This is deadly serious stuff."

Jonah looked at her sheepishly. "Sorry, love. Just with this…this virus being called vPox and all, what do you expect? Somebody's bound to call it that."

"No," Colleen said firmly. "The *apoxalypse* is all yours. Trust me on that."

For the next few minutes, the couple continued to pack in silence, Jonah tossing his clothes into his backpack while Colleen carefully folded hers, arranging them neatly in her pack. The items she decided weren't worth taking with her, she discarded on the floor beside her. At the top of the heap were her frilly pink top with the plunging cleavage and the pair of matching high heels.

"Ah no, love," Jonah said in alarm when he spotted them. "Yer not leaving the hot stuff behind, are yeh?"

Colleen frowned. "Jonah, they're not practical. We're in the middle of a full blown apocalypse. Franklin Horton is an expert on survival gear. When packing, he advises to—"

"I don't give a monkey's what Franklin Horton says," Jonah fumed, "nor Arthur bleedin' Bradley for that matter." Walking around the bed, he seized her top and heels and stuffed them into his own rucksack. "The hot stuff stays. If we don't take it with us, it really will be the end of the world. Mine anyway."

CHAPTER 27

The following morning, the Camp Knox group, as they'd chosen to call themselves, sat in the living room for their "daily brief". This was their second meeting, and Chris kept it shorter than the previous day – no more than a quick update on what was going on at the camp. With his enthusiasm and high energy personality, Cody had to admit he didn't find his talks in the least bit boring.

"Just a couple more items," Chris said, wrapping things up. He consulted his notes, then looked over at Cody and smiled. "It appears we have a sharpshooter in our midst. As you're all aware, yesterday Eddy and Cody went out on the group's first hunting expedition. Cody proved to be a superb hunter. Not only did he bag a two hundred and fifty pound buck, but he field dressed the kill like a real pro." He shot Eddy a look. "Seems like our security chief got well and truly owned."

An uncomfortable expression came over Eddy's face. Catching Cody staring at him, he glowered, instantly dispelling the initial sympathy Cody felt for him. Something told him they were never going to be friends. No loss to Cody, that was for sure.

"All right, final thing." Chris turned his attention to Walter. "As we discussed yesterday, our initial agreement was that you, Cody, and Pete would tag along with the group until we all got to know one another better. Having consulted privately with everybody, I'm pleased to announce that we are more than happy for the three of you to join us on a permanent basis." He flashed one of his beaming smiles. "It's up to you guys to decide whether you feel likewise. If so, we can go about the process of officially integrating you into the group, something I've delayed doing until now."

"What does that entail exactly?" Walter asked. "We've willingly participated in everything so far. I'm not sure what else can be expected of us."

"Walter, I'm not talking about participation, I said *integration*. That means formally submitting your supplies and equipment, just like every other member here has done."

Walter's eyebrows shot up. "Submit our supplies and equipment? Like what exactly?"

"Everything. Your food, your hunting and fishing gear, also your trucks, trailers, and weapons. Not your personal handguns, but everything else needs to—"

"Our trucks and trailers? Are you serious?" Pete broke in, an incredulous look on his face. "You really expect us to hand everything we own over to you?"

"Not to me, to the group," Chris replied coolly. "This is a survival community. Therefore, by definition, all items of survival need to belong to the community."

Cody glanced at Walter, whose frown had deepened. "That logic makes no sense to me," he said. "No reason why people can't be part of this group yet continue to have their own possessions." He looked around the room. "Really? Everyone here has handed everything over to Chris?"

A series of murmurs and nods followed. "It makes for a stronger group," Liz said, looking earnestly at Walter. "Knowing that we're all here for one another."

"No room for selfishness at Camp Knox. One hundred percent commitment," Tim said sternly. "Everything we do is for the good of the group."

Walter scratched his head. "That's a big ask," he said finally. "We'll need to think about it."

Chris smiled. "No problem. I'll give you a couple of days." He snapped his notebook shut and stood up. "All right, people, that wraps up today's brief. We all know what we need to do. Let's get on with it."

Slightly dazed, Cody stood up and left the room, accompanied by Walter and Pete. Walking out of the lodge and into the brilliant sunshine, Walter pulled the two of them over to one side. "We need to talk," he said in a tight voice. "Like straight away."

"No kidding," Pete replied.

The three headed along the lake shore until they were several hundred yards away from the lodge and out of earshot.

"That settles it for me," Walter said as soon as they'd sat down by a group of rocks overlooking the lake. "By making sure all property belongs to the group, not any individual, it gives Chris absolute power here. That's not something I can accept." He shook his head. "Damn, I should have seen that coming."

"We need to get out of here," Pete said, a worried look on his face. "I just hope there's no trouble when we do."

Walter nodded. "We need to be real careful. Let's not tell anyone of our plans until we're good and ready. Agreed?"

"Agreed," Pete replied.

"I don't get it," Cody said. "How the hell did he get everyone to agree to join on those terms?"

Walter shrugged. "Unlike the three of us, everyone else joined individually. Think about it. You're alone in a city with gangs forming around you. You're scared as hell. Someone offers to protect you…what you going to do?"

An uncomfortable look came over Pete's face. "I guess I was guilty of something worse. I was fool enough to join Mason's gang. Man, what the hell was I thinking?"

"Forget it, buddy," Walter said. "You came through in the end. Big time."

Pete perked up a little at Walter's words. "Anyway, the three of us, we're not on our own. He must be crazy if he thinks we're just going to hand our gear over to him."

"How about you, kid?" Walter asked Cody. "You've gone a little quiet. You okay about leaving here?"

Cody hesitated. Even though he still didn't know her well, the thought of leaving Emma behind played on his mind. Over the past couple of days, they'd spent a lot of time together, becoming increasingly more comfortable with one another. Cody felt there was a real chemistry between them.

"Of course," he said. "When do we go?"

"Right now, I say," Pete said.

Walter looked pensive a moment. "We got a couple of days. Let's plan a few things first."

"Like what?" Cody asked, relieved they wouldn't be going right away.

"Like finding a new camp. Don't know about you two, but I like it around here. The Cohutta is plenty big enough for another group. We just need to find the right spot, that's all."

"If they'll take us, how about moving over to the Benton camp?" Cody said. "I'm pretty sure the sheriff would love to have a guy like you around." He grinned at Pete. "Not so sure how he might feel about taking in a couple of lowly gravediggers though."

"At least you can hunt," Pete said glumly. "I haven't figured out yet what I'm good for."

Walter shook his head. "The Bentons are a tight community. They've all known each other for years. I'm not sure how well we'd fit in there. I say we start our own community."

"Just the three of us?" Pete said doubtfully.

"To start with. Then we do what Chris and Mason have done. We recruit."

Cody liked the idea immediately. "Only we do it properly. No dictators," he said, his eyes lighting up.

"Exactly," Walter said. "A community that's set up fair and square, where everyone gets their say."

Cody and Pete glanced at one another, nodding their heads in agreement. It went without saying who the leader of the new group would be.

"Let's get going on this right away," Walter continued. "We can start by moving out some of our gear. Just in case."

"In case of what?" Cody asked.

"In case Chris isn't too keen on us taking it all with us. Not saying that's going to happen, but why take the chance?"

"How about the radios?" Pete asked. "You think he'll give them back?"

Walter shrugged. "I doubt it. No point on kicking up a fuss about them. Let's just call that a parting gift. I've got a couple of sites in mind for a new camp. I'll show you them on the map later. On our afternoon break, we'll discreetly pack up some of our gear, drive out, and take a look at them, then we decide which is the most suitable. Tomorrow we'll haul more gear over. The following day, we say our goodbyes and move out."

Chris had designated three to five p.m. each day as the group's afternoon break, when people could take care of personal things. Given the oppressive summer heat the previous day, many had chosen to take a nap. Cody had chosen to spend the time with Emma.

"Sound like a plan?" Walter asked, staring at the two.

"Damn straight, it sounds like a plan," Pete said excitedly. "Looks like we'll have our very own group soon. We'll need to come up with a name for it. Any ideas?"

Walter grinned. "Anything but Camp Three Amigos. Not a lot of room for expansion there."

The three stood up and headed back to the lodge. Along the way, Cody thought about Emma. In a couple of days, he'd be leaving Camp Knox. If anything was going to happen between them, it would need to be soon.

CHAPTER 28

Russ Willis stood leaning against the door in Mason's apartment, clutching his motorcycle helmet in one hand. Unshaven, he looked even more bedraggled than the last time Mason had seen him. Two days of sleeping rough in the forest would do that. Not that Mason gave a damn. He only cared about the news Russ brought with him.

With the stink of death and garbage everywhere, compounded by the summer heat, Mason was impatient to leave Knoxville. Over the past few days, he and his gang had been busy gathering as much weapons, ammunition, and supplies as they could find.

"So…" he said, staring at Russ, "what have you learned since I last saw you? Are Walter and his friends still up at the lake?"

Russ nodded. "It's like I thought, they've set up a permanent camp at Wasson Lodge. It's a great setup. Plenty of fish in the lake, and the hunting is good too. The young kid, Walter's friend? He drove out of camp yesterday. Came back a few hours later with a big-ass deer. Must be plenty of them in the forest."

Or maybe the boy was just a good hunter, Mason thought sourly, remembering how three of his gang got taken out that night at the Chevron station. He put the distasteful thought out of his mind.

"Who's the leader of this group?" he asked. "Is it Walter?"

"No, it's a younger guy. He's got blond hair and dresses all preppy. Wears polo shirts and yachting shoes. Got plenty of energy though. He's got them working like beavers all day long."

"Yeah? Doing what exactly?"

"Gathering firewood, setting up shower stalls by the lake, stuff like that. There's even a laundry area there. Every day, people go out scavenging. They come back with their pickups loaded with all sorts of shit."

"How about security? What's the setup?"

"There's two roadblocks, not one, like I thought. They've set them up north and south of the two camps with guards posted 24/7. They've been turning plenty of other survivors away too."

"That a problem?" Mason asked, frowning.

Russ grinned. "Not for us. I've found a forest track that'll take us all the way to the lodge."

Mason looked at him keenly. "No one guarding it?"

Russ shook his head. "They've laid tripwire around the camp though. It cuts right across the track."

Mason raised an eyebrow. "Tripwire?"

"Fishing line with empty tin cans tied to it," Russ explained. "Kicks up a racket anytime someone catches their foot in it. Don't worry, I watched them put it down. I know exactly where it is."

"Good," Mason grunted. "What else?"

"A truck arrived back at the lodge yesterday full of sandbags. They've set up defensive posts around the building and posted guards."

"Who's organizing all this? That the yuppie guy too…or Walter?"

"Nope, that was another guy." Russ reached into his jacket pocket and took out a notepad. With grubby fingers, he flicked through the pages, then handed it to Mason. "I got it all figured out."

Mason stared at a neat diagram of Wasson Lodge and the surrounding area. On it, both roadblocks and several forest trails were marked. So was the line of tripwire and the camp's sandbag positions.

He looked up. "You sure nobody saw you while you were there?"

"No way," Russ said emphatically. "I'm real good at that sneaking around shit."

"How about the group at the YMCA camp? What did you find out there?" With the two camps in apparent cooperation, Mason needed to know the size of their group. They wouldn't be too happy when Mason took the lodge.

Russ hesitated. "It's well guarded, so I didn't get that close. I didn't want to risk being seen."

"I told you I needed you to find out the size of their force too," Mason said, glaring at him.

"It's okay, Mason, I did that," Russ said hurriedly. "I just mean I couldn't get close enough to map out their positions. There's thirty-odd people there, as best as I can tell."

Mason frowned. Thirty people was far bigger than his own crew. He needed to be careful tangling with a group that size.

"Yesterday, they brought up a digger and built foxholes along their perimeter," Russ continued. "They got people guarding the lake front too. I spotted them this morning on recon."

"What's got them so paranoid?"

Russ shrugged. "Just protecting what they got, I guess. There's other groups roaming around, all looking to find somewhere good to set up camp."

"Yeah, I hear you." Mason's two other scouts had come back with similar reports. There was plenty of land available, but the good locations were being snapped up fast.

"Mason, storming the lodge will be a piece of cake," Russ said earnestly. "We'll take it over before they even know what's hit them."

It was obvious how much Russ wanted Mason to take his gang to the Cohutta. It would increase his standing in the gang considerably. From the reports Mason had received from the scouts he'd sent to the Daniel Boone and Shawnee national forests, the situation on the ground was similar there. There was a bonus on going to the Cohutta, however. *Walter.*

He looked at Russ. "All right. Have you figured out a place we can stay when we get there? Somewhere no one is going to see us?"

Russ thought for a moment. "Old Fort. It's another town ten miles south of Ocoee." He grinned delightedly. "Shit, Mason. I can't wait to see Walter's face when he sees us again."

An unpleasant smile came over Mason's face. "He's got some serious payback coming his way. So do his two friends."

CHAPTER 29

With the heat of the afternoon sun on his bare back, Cody guided the two-man kayak into one of the dozens of secluded bays dotting the area around the shores of Lake Ocoee. After a few more strokes of the paddle, he let the boat glide through the reedy shallows until it scraped up to the shoreline. Once Emma had stepped off, he got out and dragged the boat out of the water until the entire hull rested on a patch of scraggy grassland.

It was another scorching day. Dressed in a T-shirt, shorts, and flip flops, Emma stood ankle deep in the water. "Good work, sailor. Let's get out of the sun and rest up awhile before heading back to camp."

"Aye aye, Captain," Cody said, giving her a goofy salute.

The two were on their afternoon break. Earlier, Walter decided it mightn't look good if all three headed out together in search of their new camp. Cody had immediately volunteered to stay behind, and as soon as Walter and Pete left, went off to find Emma. Ten minutes later, they were on the lake.

The two headed over to a nearby tree and sat down, thankful to get into the shade. Settling down on the grass shoulder to shoulder, Emma stretched out her long, tanned legs in front of her. Cody did a poor job of keeping his eyes off them.

She peered into the plastic bucket that she'd carried over. Inside were two catfish and a wide mouth bass they'd caught earlier.

"I'm so glad you invited me out here," she said, flicking a fly off her face. "I haven't gone fishing since I was a kid."

"Me too." Cody hesitated a moment, deciding what to say next. Until now, neither of the two had brought up the subject of the morning's meeting. They had been too busy enjoying themselves, diving off the kayak and into the lake's cool waters as well as fishing. Neither of them had wanted to bring the subject up and spoil the fun.

He sensed that now was the time, though. "What did you make of today's meeting?" he asked. "Me, Walter, and Pete have a big decision to make soon."

A look of concern instantly came over Emma's face. "I know. When I joined Chris, I was all on my own. It's different for you three."

"We're not sure yet what to do. It's a hard call."

She squeezed his arm. "If you decide to leave, take me with you, okay?"

He stared at her in surprise. "You mean that? You'd come with me?"

"Of course! You really think I want to stay here if you leave?"

A warm emotion stirred inside Cody. "Emma, I guess I better tell you…we're leaving soon. Right now, Walter and Pete are out scouting for a new camp."

Emma's eyes widened. "Really?"

Cody nodded. "They're looking at a few spots over on the north side of the lake, then they're going to check out a place in the mountains south of here. After that, we'll make up our minds which location is best."

Emma frowned. "How come you didn't go with them? Don't you want a say in the matter?"

"It would have looked too obvious if all three of us left together. We don't want anyone to know our plans until we're ready. Anyway, I thought it'd be better to spend more time with you. I wasn't sure whether you'd choose to come with me or not. This is all happening pretty fast."

Emma put her hand on his bare leg, leaving it to rest there. "Well, now you know," she said softly.

He stared at her, feeling the energy between them intensify. There was no mistaking it. His heart beat fast as he leaned his head slowly forward and kissed her. Immediately, Emma placed her other arm around his waist, pulling him in closer.

They kissed long and hard while time melted away. Cody wasn't aware who broke off first, but eventually they both pulled back.

Emma was the first to speak. "I've been looking forward to that for quite a while," she said, smiling.

"Me too," Cody replied, smiling as well.

They kissed again, even longer this time, then Emma pushed him gently away. "All right, sailor. You ready to row me back to camp?"

"Uh, sure," Cody said, disappointed she wanted to leave so soon. For him, things were only getting started.

"I was thinking…maybe we ought to flunk off work this afternoon and spend time in your trailer. I'd invite you to mine, but I'm not sure how Liz might feel about that."

"Sounds like a great idea. Let's just hope Comrade Chris doesn't find out about it. He might put us in front of a firing squad."

Emma giggled. "I guess that's the risk we'll have to take. These are dangerous times."

Cody stood to his feet and reached down, offering her his hand. After he pulled her up, Emma picked up the bucket and the two walked back to the kayak. Around them, the late afternoon sun sparkled off the pristine blue surface of the lake. A little lightheaded, Cody pulled the boat back into the water and the two got in.

Rowing hard, they headed back in the direction of the camp. Flunking off the rest of the afternoon with Emma seemed like the most perfect plan in the world to Cody right then.

CHAPTER 30

Deep in the Cohutta, Walter powered his Tundra down a narrow twisting road. Next to him sat Pete, while stacked full to the brim in the truck bed was a selection of camping gear, ammunition, food, and water they'd taken with them to set up an initial camp. Just in case.

They headed south, in the direction of the Tennessee-Georgia border, toward a location twenty miles south of Camp Knox known as Jack's River Falls. According to a brochure Walter had found at the lodge, it had been a popular hiking area prior to the pandemic, with dramatic scenery and a series of stunning waterfalls.

Earlier, they had been on the north side of the lake to discover that all the good spots had been taken. On top of that, there were many roving gangs in the area. At one of the camps they stopped in at, they were told that Route 74 was getting more dangerous with each passing day. Starting off with such a small group, Walter knew they had to be careful. He hoped that being in a remote area, Jack's River would prove to be a more tranquil location. Since they'd left the lake area, there'd been no passing traffic or signs of any survivor settlements yet, giving him reason for optimism.

"Cody was pretty quick to pull out of this trip," he remarked to Pete. "That's not like him to miss out on the excitement."

Pete chuckled. "There's a good reason for that. In case you hadn't noticed, there's a certain other person at the camp he's been hanging around with lately, other than us old timers."

"Been too busy to notice. Tell me."

"Ever since we arrived here, he's been spending time with that girl, Emma. Can't blame him either. She sure is pretty."

The creases on Walter's face broke into a big smile. "Damn, the kid's got taste, don't he?"

"Yup. Told me he's been hot on her since the first day he set eyes on her."

"He never said nothing to me about that," Walter said with a mock scowl. "How come I'm the one to get left out of the loop?"

Pete grinned. "Because you didn't get put on burial duty, that's why. See, us gravediggers like a good old gossip while we're busy disposing of bodies. Helps keep our minds off the work at hand."

The Tundra emerged out of thick forest and into a small valley. To either side of the road was open farmland where the forest had been cut back, and Walter spotted several ponds. "Even better than I thought," he said, pleased.

They passed a group of farm buildings on their right. A few hundred yards farther, the road dipped down to where a simple concrete bridge spanned a large river. "That's the Conasauga," he said, driving down. "On the other side is the state of Georgia. Least, it used to be. Those boundaries don't mean a damn anymore."

Crossing the river, the valley floor opened up with even more farmland on either side. "Not a single soul in sight," he said with a relieved sigh.

"Man, this is great!" Pete exclaimed. He punched Walter lightly on the shoulder. "I think we've found the perfect place."

"This is it, all right." Walter pulled up to a stop. "The area is called the Alaculsy Valley. Though you can't see it from here, we're at the bisection of two major trout streams, the Conasauga and Jack's River.

"There's so much space," Pete said, gazing to either side. "I think we need to start recruiting pronto."

"For sure. How about we put you in charge of that?" Walter opened the door to the truck. "Let's take a look around. We need to find somewhere good to hide our gear." He grinned at Pete. "I think Cody's going to be real happy when he sees this place. Who knows, he might even invite his girl out here too."

CHAPTER 31

Colleen watched while Jonah loaded the last of the supplies into the bed of their spanking new, silver Nissan Frontier, parked outside the Sun Ray Hotel. At dawn that morning, they had headed out and gotten something a little more *rugged*, as she had described it, ditching the rented Ford Taurus.

"Perfect for the ruggedly handsome guy," Jonah had said at the Nissan showroom, grinning cheekily at her.

Neither of two had driven a pickup before. Back in Dublin, the couple owned an old Toyota Corolla, a real banger. The Frontier was something different altogether. A compact four-door pickup, it was more maneuverable than a full-size truck, yet still had the strong off-road capabilities that would be required of it – according to the brochure, anyway.

Jonah climbed in behind the wheel and started the engine. "Ah now, that's a proper motor," he said for about the umpteenth time, listening to the immaculate purr of the engine. "I can't think why we didn't have one of these back home, love. We must have been crazy."

"I can't either," Colleen replied dryly, getting into the front passenger seat beside him. "Other than being short twenty thousand quid."

Jonah grinned. "Yeah, I suppose there was that. All right, I'll drive, you navigate. Take it from the top. Where do we go from here?"

Colleen rested her Armalite M-15 on the floor, the rifle stock jammed between her legs. Reaching forward, she opened the glove box and took out the road map they'd found at the showroom.

"We need to drive north on Kirkman until we get to the 408, then head east and pick up Interstate 4. That'll take us all the way to Daytona Beach." She folded the map again. "When we get there, I'll give you more directions."

Jonah grinned at her. "Right, let's hoof it. Can't wait to get to somewhere cooler. It'll do wonders for me jock itch, been driving me crazy lately." He slammed his foot on the accelerator and with a mighty roar, the Nissan shot up the road.

A few minutes later, they reached the 408 and headed east toward downtown Orlando where, at a complicated cloverleaf junction, Jonah took the correct exit, bringing them onto the I-4 heading north. To either side of them, Orlando was a ghost town. It appeared that they were among the very last survivors to leave the city.

Colleen leaned back in her seat and stole an affectionate glance at her husband who, with an eager look of anticipation on his handsome freckled face, cradled his muscular forearms around the steering wheel like a gorilla.

Though perhaps not endowed with the most critical faculties in the world, Colleen knew why she loved him so much. Jonah was tough and fearless. With a heart of pure gold, his amiable disposition and effervescent personality had ensured that in the four years since he'd first chatted her up while they stood in line at a lunchtime deli counter, Colleen in her trim office outfit, Jonah in workman's overalls, she'd never once been bored with the man. He had, however, often driven her crazy on more occasions than she could recall.

Turning her gaze toward the miles of sprawling freeway ahead, she took a moment to assess their situation.

Over the course of the past few days, it had gone from *bleedin' woeful,* to one where they at least stood a chance, their destiny firmly in their own hands. The pickup was stocked to the brim with every conceivable item they would need for their survival, and thanks to Dr. Bradley's detailed description on how to drain gasoline from underneath a vehicle, they had a tank full of gas and the tools to drain more along the way.

Though there was no direction home, with Jonah's brawn and her brains, she felt confident they could survive this. It was merely a question of staying tough and not making any stupid mistakes.

CHAPTER 32

All morning, Cody was kept busy digging post holes for the new perimeter fence. It was another sweltering day. The sky was blue, the sun punishing, and the work grueling. Knowing that he would be leaving the next day, his heart wasn't in it, and his mind constantly floated onto other matters, specifically, their new camp. And Emma.

The previous day, the two had spent the entire afternoon in his trailer, not emerging until suppertime, when they had walked separately up to the lodge.

In the dining room, Pete had given him a sly wink. His trailer was next to his, and Cody guessed he'd heard them talking. "New place looks good," Pete whispered to him. "Day after tomorrow, we're outta here."

Later that evening, he and Walter filled Cody in on the details. Afterward, Pete had said, "All right kid, seeing as we're leaving tomorrow, is there anything in particular you need to talk to me and Walter about? Spit it out, kid. Nothing like a bit of gossip to pass the time, right Walter?"

Gratefully, Cody took Pete's cue to tell the two all about Emma, relieved when neither had objected to her coming with them. On the contrary, both had been delighted to sign up their first recruit for the new camp.

***

He was pouring gravel into a post hole when he heard the shrill sound of whistles from somewhere nearby. Whistles had been issued to the guards on duty and was the camp's emergency signal.

Clutching his rifle, Cody sprinted up to the lodge. His assigned battle station was a sandbag position on the southwest corner of the building. The previous day, several blinds had been built with interlocking fields of fire. Eddy had bowed to Walter's superior tactical knowledge and allowed him to mark out the positions.

Before Cody reached his post, the whistles stopped blowing, ending with a series of short pips indicating the emergency was over. He arrived to see three strangers at the front of the building. Two were men, each standing beside a Harley Davidson motorbike, while a woman stood next to the bigger of the two men. He was extremely tall, perhaps six foot five.

As he got closer, Cody got the chance to observe him better. He had tightly-cropped black hair and wore motorcycle leathers. Lean, with piercing black eyes, he looked tough as nails. Slung over his back was an automatic rifle, and on his left hip he carried a pistol.

The most distinguishing feature about him, however, was his grossly disfigured face. Both cheeks had deep scars etched across them, a long slash ran across the top of his forehead, and yet another set of scars crisscrossed his chin.

Similarly armed, his companion was far smaller. Bucktoothed, of average height, he had sandy hair cut pudding bowl style, a small goatee, and wore baggy jeans and a short-sleeved camouflage shirt. His pale blue eyes stared around at the gathering group warily.

The woman appeared to be armed with only one pistol, which she carried in a shoulder holster over a tight-fitting T-shirt. She was incredibly beautiful. Long legged, she had shoulder-length hair with expensive-looking highlights, and smooth translucent skin with slightly hooded eyes that hinted of something Asian.

A pucker of a smile played on her lips, like she was amused by all the commotion the three had caused. Despite being surrounded by Eddy and three other armed men, none of them looked in the least bit scared.

Cody spotted Chris hurrying over from the lake. "Who the hell let these people in?" he said angrily when he reached the lodge. "No one is allowed past the roadblock without my permission." He spotted their weapons. "And why do they still have their guns?"

"They refused to hand them over," Eddy told him, looking embarrassed. "They didn't come past the roadblock. Mark caught them riding past his guard post. They must have sneaked in through the forest."

Mark nodded vigorously, delighted to be involved in the unfolding drama. Along with James, he seemed to spend most of his time on guard duty, though neither man appeared to mind.

"Hey, we didn't sneak nowhere!" the bucktoothed intruder protested.

"Absolutely not," the woman said calmly. "Or we wouldn't have stopped right away when your men asked us to."

"Even though their damn whistles practically deafened us," Scarface said sourly, reaching a hand up to his ear and rubbing it.

Puffing out his chest, Chris strode up to him. Barely coming up to his shoulder, Cody couldn't help but think how comical it looked. If he chose to, Scarface could have swatted him away like a fly.

"Who the hell are you? You've no right to be here. And why would you ride up through the forest unless you were trying to sneak in?"

Scarface's lip curled up into a sneer. Before he could reply, the woman pointed to the smaller man. "Because Clete here is from these parts," she explained. "He brought us through the forest from Devil's Point."

Clete nodded proudly. "Sure did. I know this area like the back of my hand. Been hunting and fishing around here my whole damned life."

"Really? Where is your camp?" Chris asked.

"Nowhere yet. We just drove up from Atlanta this morning."

Chris glanced at the two motorbikes. "You three came all the way from Atlanta with no gear?" he said suspiciously. "That doesn't make sense."

"We drove up in pickups," Clete explained. "Parked them down at the Point, then rode up here on our bikes. We were planning on making the lodge our new home."

There was a frown on Chris's face as he digested all this. "I guess I'll just have to take that on face value. But as you can see, this is *our* home. You'll need to move on and find somewhere else."

"Plenty of other places for us to go, mister" Scarface growled. He threw a leg over the side of his Harley, then indicated for the woman to get on behind him.

By this stage, practically the entire camp had crowded around the three strangers. Scarface waved a hand dismissively at them. "Make some space and we'll be on our way. No need to chase us out like common criminals."

"Common criminals!" Clete said with a wheezy laugh, mounting his machine. "That's funny, Ralph."

Walter stepped out in front of the motorcycles. "Now wait a minute," he said, looking around at the group. "Is it just me, or are we being darned unfriendly? Three people on their own are going to run into trouble real fast around here, particularly seeing as one of them is a woman. Is there any reason why they can't stay a few days until they get their bearings?"

"Because I just ordered them off my land," Chris said, glowering at Walter. "That's why."

"This land belongs to the group, not *you*," Walter corrected him. "Remember?"

"Of which I am the leader," Chris snapped back. "So I get to make the decision."

Greta, whose tall, angular figure stood near the back of the group spoke up. "Walter is right, Chris," she said in her customary sharp tone. "For heaven's sake, show our fellow survivors some hospitality. We wouldn't even be here ourselves if the Benton group hadn't shown us some kindness and let us through."

"Only because they need Walter's skills," Chris retorted. "They were about to turn us away otherwise."

"Well now, I'm sure we can use Clete's skills," Walter said, throwing him a wink. "I'm betting he knows all the best fishing spots around here."

"Hell yes!" Clete exclaimed. "In fact, I know a great little trout stream real close by. I'd be happy to show you it."

"And hunting," Cody chimed in. "I'd like his opinion on that too."

Clete glanced over at him. From the look on his face, Cody could tell he was relishing all the attention he was getting. "Happy to do that, son. Nothing I like better than to talk about hunting. Best done over a glass of whiskey, of course," he added with a roguish grin.

"That can be arranged," Cody said grinning back. Despite his rough appearance, there was something immediately likable about Clete, and while Ralph looked downright scary, it appeared his girlfriend had some control over him.

"Chris," Walter said reasonably, "I'm in favor of making friends, not enemies, whenever I can. No reason why we can't all be good neighbors. So how about a little mutual cooperation here?"

Out-argued by three of his own group, Chris relented. He didn't look happy about it, though. "All right," he said gruffly. "They can stay a couple of days until they find somewhere suitable."

From the look on Ralph's face, it appeared he was about to turn down Chris's ungracious offer. Sitting behind him on the Harley, the girl spoke up before he could. "Thank you, we appreciate that. I, for one, look forward to getting to know you all."

Chris's demeanor softened. "You better bring your pickups here right away, before somebody steals them. I'll radio down to the guards at the roadblock to let you through." With a curt nod, he headed back toward the lake.

**

A short time later, Walter, Pete, and Cody sat three-in-a-row on camping stools outside Pete's trailer. Before the strangers left to fetch their vehicles, Walter had briefly introduced himself and suggested they bring their trailers over to the west side of the camp where there was plenty of room.

"I'm surprised you're in favor of allowing those three to stay here. They're pretty rough-looking," Pete said to Walter, staring at him curiously. "The men, I'm talking about. That Maya can stay as long as she likes. She's a real looker."

Walter chuckled. "If ever I saw a couple that resembled Beauty and the Beast, that's them right there. But like I said, no point in making enemies for no good reason."

Pete continued to stare at him. "That it? I think you're holding out on me, partner."

Walter grinned. "You're getting to know me too well. Seeing as we're about to leave, I thought I might fuck with Chris a little. Couldn't help myself. Anyway, some fresh people around here might wake the others up. So far, most of them are walking around like hypnotized chickens. Except for Greta, that is."

Pete laughed. "It'd take a lot to hypnotize Ralph. For a start, Chris would need to stand up on a stool."

**

196

Down at the lake, Ralph leaned against the side of his pickup, smoking a cigarette and staring out across the water. The trio had just returned to Devil's Point, this time riding down the lodge's main driveway, then turning south onto the Cookson Creek Road where, at the roadblock – the one they'd been completely unaware of – they'd been waved through by two armed men.

They had ridden up from Atlanta that morning in their F-150 pickups. The drive had been uneventful. Reaching the town of Ocoee, Clete guided them along the back roads to Devil's Point, where he'd suggested that they ride their Harleys through the forest up to the lodge.

Ralph took another drag of his cigarette before speaking. "That Chris is a real asshole. I'd be happy to blow him off, but we'll be safer at the lodge until we figure this out. Best not to take any chances." After the incident in the Hilton the previous evening, he had no intention of being that sloppy again.

"Absolutely," Maya agreed. "Other than Chris, the rest of them seem all right. Beats me why they elected him as their leader."

"Maybe he elected himself. Seems the type." Ralph flicked his cigarette into the lake. "All right, we stay a couple of days until we get the lay of the land. Clete, you need to figure out this boonie shit real fast," he growled.

Maya smiled at Clete. "Us city slickers are counting on you, Mr. Hillbilly. Don't let us down."

CHAPTER 33

Two hundred and eighty miles out of Orlando, the Nissan Frontier cruised at seventy miles an hour up Interstate 95. Jacksonville was in the rear mirror, with Savannah the next major city the Irish couple would pass. Jonah had been solid at the wheel for nearly four hours straight, anxious for them to leave the south as soon as they could. He couldn't wait to reach a more bearable climate.

He stared at the fuel gauge. "Colleen, we're running low on juice," he told her. "We'll need to pull off the freeway soon and drain more gas. Can't wait to roll under another car and splash petrol all over me face again."

Colleen grinned. "Smells better than your aftershave." She consulted the map. "We're coming up to a town called Richmond Hill. We can exit there."

"All right, let's see if we can find another Chevy pickup. Stick to what we know, eh?" The vehicle Jonah had previously drained had been a Chevy Silverado. There was more space to work underneath a pickup than a sedan, making the task easier.

Ten minutes later, they pulled off I-95 at exit 87, taking the off ramp down to the T-junction of a large highway. Turning right, they passed a Motel 6 on one side of the road, a Travelodge directly opposite it. Next came a

Domino's Pizza joint, followed by a Waffle House, then a Denny's, and a Smoking Pig.

"Smoking Pig?" Jonah chuckled. "Didn't see them in Orlando. Ah well, missed me chance now."

"Focus on the job at hand," Colleen scolded him. "We're here to collect fuel."

Ahead on the far side of the highway was a Food Lion supermarket. Jonah spotted movement in the parking lot. "Hey, there's people over there, look!"

He pointed across the road, straining his neck to get a better view to where a group of men stood by a red pickup. They stared back at the Nissan as it drove by.

"Keep going," Colleen said in a tight voice. "I don't like the look of them."

At that moment, a woman darted into view from behind the men. She ran across the lot and headed toward the grass embankment that bordered the highway. She had long brown hair and wore a T-shirt and jeans. As Jonah drove past, she waved a hand desperately at him, a pleading look on her face.

Two of the men had sprinted after her. One caught up with her as she ran between two trees and out onto the road. Seizing her roughly by the hair, he dragged her up the grass incline again and back into the parking lot.

"Oh my God!" Colleen exclaimed. "That poor woman. Jonah, what are we going to do?"

Jonah put his foot down on the pedal, and the Nissan immediately picked up speed. "We're minding our own business, that's what. There's at least five of them. We got to put ourselves first."

"Really?" Colleen asked uncertainly.

"Yeah, really."

The pickup sped down the highway at ninety miles an hour. Half a mile farther was a junction with a turnoff for an Argos store on their right. Jonah slowed down, pulled into the entranceway, and came to a screeching halt. "Or at least, that's what we want them to think."

"So we're going back?"

Jonah faced Colleen, a grim look of determination etched on his features. "Look, love, remember the geezer who saved our lives the other day when we were out shopping?"

Colleen nodded.

"We're going to do the same. I couldn't live with meself otherwise."

Colleen buzzed down her window. "Me neither." She grabbed her M-15 and stuck the barrel out the window. "Come on. We need to be quick about this."

Jonah backed out onto the freeway, crossing the junction and onto the far side of the road. He threw the vehicle into drive and headed back toward the Food Lion.

"All right, here's the plan. Soon as we get to the car park, you start shooting with all you got. I'll head straight for those bastards and mow down as many as I can, all right?"

Colleen looked at him nervously. "All right, but the entrance to the supermarket is on the far side of the lot. They're going to get plenty of warning we're coming."

"Don't worry. I got that covered."

The Nissan zoomed down a dip in the road. Coming up the far side, Jonah steered around a long bend to see the supermarket come into view on their right. He got as far over on the left hand side of the highway as he could, then increased his speed.

When they reached the embankment bordering the supermarket lot, he swerved across the road and headed for it, trying to get as straight an angle as he possibly could. The wheels clattered over the low curb and raced up the side of the incline. Moments later, the Nissan sailed over the top, all four wheels in the air.

"*Jonaaah!*" Colleen screeched.

"*Jaysuuus!*" Jonah screamed.

With a jolt, the front wheels hit the concrete, followed a moment later by the back wheels.

Jonah tugged hard at the wheel, trying desperately to control the vehicle. Miraculously, he weaved it safely through a group of abandoned cars.

Straight ahead was the red pickup where the group of men stood. Seeing him approach, they scattered in all directions across the lot. Some already had their pistols out and began firing.

"Shoot the fuckers!" Jonah yelled.

Colleen opened fire, repeatedly pulling the trigger to release a stream of bullets at the men. One on Jonah's right fell to the ground, while two others ducked around the back of a group of cars.

To his left, he spotted the woman. She was being dragged by the hair by one of the men, heading toward a motorbike parked in the middle of the lot. In his other hand, the man held a pistol.

There were no other vehicles nearby, and he had to break cover to reach the motorbike. As soon as he did, Jonah picked up speed. The man jerked his head back to see the Nissan bearing down on him. He stopped running and faced the pickup, leveling his pistol.

Taking advantage of the situation, the woman managed to break free. She stumbled to the ground, got quickly up again, and started running.

"Swing left!" Colleen cried out.

Jonah turned the wheel at a hard angle so the Nissan was broadside with the man, giving Colleen the perfect angle to fire. The M-15 spewed out a hail of bullets, several of them catching the man across his waist.

"Nice!" Jonah yelled gleefully as the man buckled, dropping to the ground.

Spinning the wheel to his right now, he drove after the fleeing woman, who was still running in the direction of the parking lot entrance. He tooted hard on the horn several times.

"Stop!" he shouted out the window.

The woman whirled around to see the stricken man on the ground and stopped running. Colleen reached a hand back and flung open the back passenger door as Jonah screeched to a halt beside the woman.

"Get in!" Colleen shouted.

The woman threw herself inside. Jonah put his foot down again and raced up to the exit. He yanked the wheel hard and turned left onto the street.

The highway junction was fifty yards away. Reaching it, he pulled onto the freeway and headed in the direction of the off-ramp they'd driven down less than ten minutes ago.

Colleen shoved her head out the window to see if any of the gang were giving chase.

"They coming after us?" Jonah asked anxiously.

Colleen shook her head. "I don't see them."

Jonah glanced quickly back at their new passenger. "You all right, missus?"

The woman nodded her head. "Yes, I'm fine," she said, still panting from her exertions. "I don't know what to say...I...I can't believe you did that."

In the mirror, Jonah grinned at her. "No problem. This is what we do." He glanced at Colleen. "Right, love?"

Colleen pulled her head away from the window to stare back at him. "*This is what we do?* Jonah, I think that's the corniest thing I've ever heard you say."

Jonah shrugged. "It's the new me, baby. Start getting used to it."

CHAPTER 34

Monica Jeffreys was a thirty-eight-year-old housewife who had lived in Richmond Hill for over fifteen years. Part of the overall Savannah Metropolitan Area, Richmond had been a quiet town prior to the pandemic. Her husband Charles, a local businessman, owned a deli and a pizza parlor at Parker Square, the town's main mall. Though she'd helped part-time with the business doing the bookkeeping and ordering supplies, Monica spent most of her time looking after their two young children, aged seven and nine. All that had changed five days ago when Charles, Jason, and Sophie all died.

There was no hospital in Richmond, the nearest one being St. Joseph's in Savannah, fifteen miles away. Monica had driven there straightaway when Sophie had first gotten sick, only to be politely but firmly turned away. By that evening, both Charles and Jason had come down with vPox symptoms. Three days later, she'd spent the entire day digging three graves in her back garden.

"I'm sorry to hear that. These are terrible times," Jonah said quietly, keeping the Nissan at a steady seventy, passing parched summer fields to either side of the highway in terrain as flat as a pancake.

They were back on I-95. Earlier, Monica had guided them through Richmond's back streets to neighboring Georgetown, where they'd pulled up behind a Mitsubishi Pajero and refilled the gas tank to the halfway setting.

Draining the Pajero had been easy. Just like on the Silverado, under the rear of the truck Jonah had found the tank's drain cock, and with a flathead screwdriver had pried the plug half out. Splashing his face and clothes, he'd slid a plastic pan underneath to catch the petrol, and after several goes, had filled up two gas cans. Perhaps Dr. Arthur Bradley wasn't such a bad geezer after all.

"How about you guys?" Monica asked. "I guess you haven't heard any news on things back in your own country?"

Jonah shook his head. "Last thing we heard was that the government closed all the borders. No one allowed in or out, either by air or sea."

"I just hope to God they shut them in time," Colleen said fervently. She sat leaning against the front passenger door so that she had a view of Monica. "It would only take one infected person to…."

Jonah patted her on the knee. "Don't think about it, love. It'll only drive you crazy." He turned to Monica. "So what's your plan? We're heading north up the coast to…to…well to somewhere less hot. Yer welcome to come with us. It's not safe for you to travel on your own."

"Thank you, but if you could help me find another vehicle, that would really be appreciated. I'm going to Tennessee. I'm originally from a small town there. Actually, I planned on leaving right after stocking up on supplies at the Food Lion…before those men tried to assault me." She shook her head. "I still can't believe it. That man you shot, I knew him. He was a neighbor of mine."

"With no one to keep the lid on things, it all turned bad real quick," Jonah replied. "But there's good people out there too. We had a guy save our bacon the other day. Crazy thing is, we never even got a chance to thank him."

"Monica," Colleen broke in, "you say you're from a small town in Tennessee…what exactly is the population?"

Monica thought for a moment. "About fifteen hundred, if memory serves me correctly."

Colleen made a quick calculation. "There can't be more than thirty-odd survivors then. Chances are you won't know many of them. Especially after fifteen years."

"I should know some of them. Charles and I used to take the kids there each summer. It's beautiful around Benton. We used to hike in the forests, go canoeing on the lake. It's where Charles taught the kids to fish." Monica bit her lip. "Such good memories."

Jonah glanced at her in the mirror. "Fish, you say?"

Monica nodded. "Plenty of bass and catfish in Lake Parkside. Lake Ocoee as it's known these days. And there's trout in the rivers, rainbow and browns. There's even brookies in some of the feeder streams."

Jonah and Colleen exchanged glances. "How about meat? Any deer there?" Colleen asked.

"Plenty. It's a popular area for hunting. There's whitetails and wild pigs. Lots of squirrels too. Charles wasn't so interested in that. He loved fishing, though."

"Sound man," Jonah said approvingly.

"Why don't you come with me?" Monica urged. "It's a good place for you two as well. Especially seeing as I know the area."

Colleen looked at Jonah. "What do you think?"

Jonah lifted a hand off the wheel and scratched his head. "I don't know, love," he said doubtfully. "I have me heart set on somewhere near the sea. Someplace I can get meself a nice fishing boat."

"Lake Ocoee is big. Everyone in the area has a boat. *Had* a boat. It sounds terrible to say, but you'll find yourself a nice one."

"Come on, Jonah. Let's try it," Colleen said. "If it doesn't work out, we can always move on."

Jonah glanced at Monica through the rearview mirror again. "What's the weather like there? We left Orlando because it's too hot." He stared down at his pink arms. "The place just doesn't suit me skin type."

Monica smiled. "It'll be hot there now, though not as bad as Florida. The winters are cold, though. Fall in particular is a beautiful time of the year."

Jonah reflected for a moment. "All right, we'll give it a shot. A boat on the lake sounds good."

Monica looked delighted. Collen smiled at her, then opened the glove compartment and took out the map.

"No need for that. I know the route," Monica told her. "From here, the quickest way is to turn back and take the 16 west. It'll be marked for Chattanooga."

Jonah's ears pricked up. "Chattanooga? Pardon me, but is that where they keep the choo choo?" he asked, imitating the sound of a train whistle. In a throaty but melodious voice, he blasted out the first couple of lines of the famous song.

Jonah loved music. Something that had been passed down from his family. Every Christmas they would gather around the table—his mother and father, uncles and aunts, nieces and nephews—and take turns belting out Irish rebel songs. Jonah had a fine voice too, especially once it had been lubricated with a few beers.

"Ah, me Da loved that choon," he said wistfully. "Used to sing it to us when we were nippers, so he did."

He veered into the right hand lane where a highway exit loomed ahead so he could turn around. He grinned. "Come on, ladies, how about a sing-song along the way? It'll make the time fly by." Picking up the song from where he'd left off, he began singing lustily again.

The two women looked at one other, then burst out laughing. "Monica, it's a long way to Tennessee," Colleen finally said. "Are you sure you're up for this?"

CHAPTER 35

That afternoon Cody lay in bed staring up at the ceiling, thinking about how Walter and Pete were getting on. An hour ago, the two had left to make a second trip to the Jack's River camp, taking with them more equipment and provisions. They were due back shortly. With the antagonism between Chris and Walter growing, it made even more sense to move more of their gear out.

"A penny for your thoughts?" Emma asked, lying naked beside him. For the second afternoon in a row she'd come over to Cody's trailer. After making love, the two had drifted off into a comfortable sleep and had just woken up.

"Just thinking about tomorrow. I hope there won't be any problems with Chris. I don't think he's going to be very happy when he sees the four of us pick up and leave." Cody glanced at her. "Especially you."

A worried look came over Emma's face. "What do Walter and Pete think about me coming with you? They okay about it?"

"They're cool. Besides, we need more people. We're looking to build a new community."

Emma smiled. "So I'm just coming along to make up the numbers, is that it?"

"That's it, it's all about the numbers! Seriously though, I think this is going to work out good. Walter is one of the smartest people I know. He's a good person too. I trust him. We can build something better than what Chris is doing here."

"That wouldn't be hard," Emma said with a snort. "He's turned into such an asshole."

"I agree. He's become so pumped up and arrogant, I've no idea why people still put up with him. Maybe one or two others might choose to come with us tomorrow."

"I don't think so," Emma said. "It's a good setup here, especially with Camp Benton so close by. It makes people feel safer."

"That makes me even happier you've chosen to come with me."

Emma brushed her fingers across his chest. "Me too, Cody."

At that moment, there were a couple of sharp raps on the door, followed by an even louder one. Cody's heart jumped. It was too aggressive to be Walter and Pete returning. Besides, he would have heard Walter's truck coming down the drive.

Clambering out of bed, he crossed over to the window and peeked out behind the blind. Standing by his trailer door were Chris and Eddy. A couple of feet behind them stood Mark and James.

"Emma, quick, get dressed," he whispered. "Chris is outside. He's got Eddy and two others with him."

Emma bolted upright in the bed. "What do they want?" she asked in alarm. She slid off the edge of the bed and began searching for her clothes.

"I don't know. Stay here. I'm going to find out."

Throwing on his shorts and a T-shirt, Cody headed over to the trailer door and opened it. A shaft of sunlight from the low afternoon sun temporarily blinded him and he raised a hand up to his eyes to shade them.

"What's up?" he said, staring down the steps at Chris.

"I think you know," Chris replied, a grim look on his face.

"Nope. Hit me with it."

"I heard you three are preparing to leave the group, that correct?"

Cody hesitated a moment before replying. "We haven't made up our minds yet. Why?"

"Don't play games," Chris snapped. "I know damned well you are. That's fine with me, just don't think you can take any of the women with you." He glared at Cody. "Liz told me Emma's been spending a lot of time with you lately. That true?"

"What the hell's that got to do with you?" Cody said angrily. "It's none of your business." He glanced over at Eddy, who stood with his arms folded and a smirk on his face, clearly relishing the drama.

"So it is true." Chris's face grew harder. "When you leave camp, the women stay. That includes Emma. Find your own damn women. If you think—"

"Don't the *damn women* have any say in this?" Emma had come to the door to stand beside Cody. She stared down the steps at Chris, a contemptuous look on her face. "When exactly did we lose the right to act for ourselves?"

The sight of Emma inside Cody's trailer had a bad effect on Chris. His face grew red, and a vein began to twitch at his temple. "Since last week, when the whole world went to Hell, that's when. Things aren't the way they were before. If women expect to be protected, they need to show a little appreciation in return."

"Anything else they need to show?" Cody asked sarcastically. "And what if one of them is more interested in a lowly gravedigger than the king? What then?"

Chris's eyes blazed. Before Cody could react, he bounded up the steps and grabbed him by both arms. Using his weight, Chris pulled him off balance and threw him down the steps. "What then? I'll show you what then!" he roared.

Cody rolled across the grass. As soon as he tried to stand up, a boot slammed into his chest, pinning him to the ground. He looked up to see Eddy standing over him. "Not so fast, *kid*," he said, an unpleasant smile on his face.

Cody grabbed his foot and struggled to get out from underneath it. At that moment, Emma screamed. He twisted his neck to see Chris lunge a foot at him, his face contorted with rage. Cody raised his arm and managed to partially deflect the blow. Still, Chris's boot caught the side of his face, sending his head spinning back.

Chris lifted his foot back and was about to kick out again when a car horn blared. He stopped and looked back. Tearing down the driveway was Walter's white Tundra. Moments later, it swerved off the path and headed across the field to pull up ten feet away.

Cody shoved Eddy's foot away and rose to his feet. By now, having heard all the commotion, several others had come to gather around the trailer, arriving from different directions of the camp. Most had bewildered looks on their faces.

Walter jumped out of the pickup and marched over to them, Pete hurrying close behind. "Cody, you all right?" Walter asked when he reached him.

Cody rubbed the side of his jaw. "Yeah, I'm fine." He glanced over at Emma, who had come down the steps of the trailer and stood a few feet away. He lowered his eyes, embarrassed how he'd let himself get caught off guard.

"Feel like picking on someone your own size, Chris?" Walter asked. He glanced over at Eddy. "Maybe without the help of your friend this time."

A confident smile spread over Chris's face. "Is that a challenge, *Walt*?" he asked mockingly. "Seems like you've been trying to undermine my authority since the day we met. Maybe you're looking to take over this camp, that it?"

"I'm looking to give you a good hiding, that's all. Soon as I'm done, I'm leaving. Cody and Pete are coming with me." Walter looked around at the watching group.

"Anyone else who wants to come with us is free to do so. Don't be afraid. Just pack up your stuff and go. Ain't no law that says different."

"No one is going anywhere," Chris said flatly. "Except for you, and that's on a stretcher. Cody and Pete can carry you out of here." He cracked his knuckles, then raised his arms into what looked like some type of martial arts pose. "Enough talk, old man. Time to settle this thing. You ready?"

Walter made no reply. Raising his arms up into a classic boxer's pose, he watched Chris warily, who began to circle him, making neat deft steps to one side, then the other.

"Oh, did I tell you? I'm a second dan in Kempo karate." Chris smiled. "It's a brutal martial art. A real bone cracker."

Cody's heart was beating hard. Though both men were about the same height and weight, Chris was at least a dozen years younger than Walter. He was far the fitter too, his body strong and athletic. Although Walter was powerfully built, it didn't look like he'd hit the gym in quite a few years, and Cody suspected he would be the slower of the two.

His fears were confirmed when Chris suddenly moved in. With lightning speed, he threw a flurry of one-two punches around Walter's face. Catching him on the nose with one, Walter retaliated with a clumsy hook that Chris easily pulled back from in time. A trickle of blood ran down Walter's chin. He brushed it away with the back of his hand, his eyes fixed on his opponent the whole time.

Chris grinned, a tense, predatory look on his face. "Too slow, old man. Something tells me you've been eating too much pork and beans lately."

Coming in again, he feinted with a punch. As Walter raised his arms to protect his face, Chris swiveled his hip and unleashed a vicious sidekick. The heel of his foot struck Walter in the belly. With a grunt, he staggered back, just in time to duck out of the way of a follow up punch. Blinking hard, Walter worked off the pain. Luckily, Chris's kick had landed on his lower stomach, not his solar plexus, otherwise he would have been doubled-up by now.

Chris glanced over at the watching crowd, grinning arrogantly. "Greta, you better fetch that stretcher. Walt is going to need it real soon."

Greta let out a contemptuous snort. "You've got a big mouth, Chris," she said, her tone sharp as a whip. "I wouldn't be so sure of that."

Chris shrugged. "We'll see."

Her comment took the shine off his mood. He came forward again, a scowl on his face, looking like he meant to finish this off. Turning his hip as if he was about to release another sidekick, instead, he stepped quickly forward and threw a ferocious straight-right punch at Walter.

There was a certain poetic beauty to what happened next. It occurred so fast, Cody almost missed it. As Chris lunged forward, Walter shifted his head slightly to one side so that the punch merely struck a glancing blow across his cheek. Stepping in, his right hand down by his waist, he swung a powerful upper hook, putting all his weight into it.

It caught Chris squarely on the jaw. His entire body crumpled on impact, like it had run into a brick wall. For all intents and purposes, it had. To the sound of astonished gasps, Chris collapsed face first to the ground in a heap where he remained motionless. Out cold.

Walter stared down at him. "For the last time, it's Walter. Oh, and another thing. Did I tell you I used to be an Army middleweight champion?" He patted his belly. "I've put on a few pounds since then. Still, you don't forget the moves."

He turned around to face the crowd, half of whose mouths still hung open. Cody's certainly did.

"All right people," he said, speaking in a calm even tone that showed no indication of his previous exertions. "Like I said, Cody, Pete, and myself are leaving Camp Knox to start our own group. We planned on going tomorrow, but something tells me it might be better to move things forward.

We've found a great spot not too far from here. As well as great hunting and fishing, there's good farmland there too, and—"

He broke off as a grim-faced Eddy walked over to Chris, who'd begun to stir. Kneeling down, Eddy reached under his armpits and lifted him to his feet.

Chris looked dazed, his eyes unfocused. "Wh-what's going on?" he mumbled, leaning heavily on Eddy. Then he spotted Walter. Slowly, it dawned on him what had occurred.

"All right folks, that's all I have to say," Walter said, wrapping up his short speech. "You're all grown men and women. You know everything you need to know to make your decision." With that, he went over to where Cody stood with Emma and Pete. "Come on," he said. "We need to hitch up our trailers and leave. Who knows how this will turn out?"

"Emma, go pack your things," Cody said. "Meet me back here in ten."

"By the way, good to have you on board," Walter said, smiling at Emma.

"Wait! I'm coming too!" Greta broke in as Emma was about to leave. She moved away from the others and came over to the small group. "I'll go fetch some medicine from the infirmary, pack my clothes, and I'll be ready." She hesitated. "I have no trailer. Someone will have to take me in for the moment."

Walter nodded. "You can take mine. Me and Pete can room together until we haul more trailers up here."

"Thank you."

Greta had turned to leave when a single shot rang out. Cody jerked his head around to see Chris standing ten feet away, his Steyr pointing in their direction. Close by, Eddy, Mark, and James likewise had their pistols trained on them.

"No one other than Walter, Cody, and Pete are going anywhere," Chris said tightly. He appeared to have recovered from his knockout blow. "You got a lucky punch in, old man. Sometimes that happens and the best man doesn't win. But it doesn't change anything. The women aren't going anywhere. Emma and Greta belong to this camp."

Not party to his previous utterances, Greta stared at him incredulously. "Chris, are you out of your mind? This isn't an Islamic Caliphate. Us women are free to do whatever we want. There's no law that can stop us."

"Greta, there's no law, period," Chris said, his voice grating. "Anyone who tries to leave this camp without my permission will be shot before they make it ten yards."

Greta's eyes widened even farther. "You really have lost it, haven't you?" A resolute frown came over her face. "I'm going to fetch my things. If you want to shoot, then shoot." Without another word, she turned around and marched off in the direction of the lodge.

Chris raised his pistol and pointed it at her retreating figure. "Come back here!" he yelled at her furiously. "I'm serious, I'll shoot!"

Before anyone could react, from behind Chris several shots rang out in quick succession. Chris spun around to see a tall figure twenty yards away, bearing down on him. It was Ralph, coming from the direction of his trailer in the far corner of the field, his rifle raised to his shoulder.

"Fuckhead, I wouldn't do that if I were you," he called out in a deep growl.

Following close behind him were Clete and Maya. Clete carried his rifle while Maya held a pistol in her grip. As they approached, people scattered in all directions, moving out of the line of fire.

"Hey, this is none of your business," Chris said angrily as the trio came to a halt ten feet away. "You're not part of this group."

"You point a gun at a woman like that, I'm making it my business," Ralph told him curtly. He stared at Eddy, Mark, and James, who stood nervously, trying to figure out what to do. "Put those pistols away or I'll riddle you full of holes."

"In fact, best thing is you boys drop them on the ground right now," Maya said calmly. "That way nobody gets hurt."

Clete had moved several feet away from Ralph to provide a separate field of fire at the three men.

Eddy looked over uncertainly at Chris. "What do you want us to do?"

"Now!" Ralph roared.

Shaking his head in frustration, Chris leaned over and dropped the Steyr on the ground, followed immediately by Eddy, Mark, and James, who all appeared relieved to do so.

Gun in hand, Maya walked over to them and collected the weapons.

Cody glanced over toward the driveway to see that Greta had reached it. A moment later, she disappeared from sight behind a row of bushes. He had to admire her stubborn pluckiness and wondered if she knew just how lucky she'd been.

Walter nodded his head in appreciation at Ralph, then faced Chris, "Were you really going to shoot Greta in the back?" he asked incredulously.

Chris made no reply. He appeared stunned by the events of the past few minutes, and how they'd all transpired against him. Cody too was dazed. Everything had happened so quickly, it was hard to take in.

"Given the right circumstance, it doesn't take long for men to show their true natures, does it?" Walter said, shaking his head. "Strip away the veil of civilization, and there they stand for all to see. There's the good, there's the bad..." he stared over at Ralph, "and there's the ugly."

Maya smiled. "While they might appear like monsters, sometimes the ugly have hearts of gold."

"True," Walter replied. He stared at the trio. "With all the confusion, you three mightn't know exactly what's going on here. There's been a parting of ways at this camp. If I was a politician, I'd chalk it up to irreconcilable differences, or something like that."

"No kidding," Ralph said.

Walter smiled. "Anyway, the upshot is that five of us are leaving right now. You three are welcome to join us."

"Where will you go?" Clete asked. "If you plan on leaving the Cohutta, count us out. Like I told you, this is my old stomping ground. Don't make sense for us to go anyplace else."

"We'll be staying in the area," Walter told him. "Come over to my trailer and I'll show you exactly where on the map. Then you can decide if you want to come with us. I, for one, would certainly like that."

"Me too," Cody said enthusiastically, Emma and Pete joining him almost in unison. They all looked at each other and burst out laughing.

Maya broke out into a smile too. "Thank you. I think we'd like that. Looks like we've got a new community forming. How exciting!"

EPILOGUE
(12 DAYS EARLIER)

By its very definition, the Level 4 Biohazard laboratory where Dr. Robert D. Clements, Ph.D. worked was not a *healthy* environment. Nor was it a comfortable one. Heat built up quickly inside the positive-pressure protective suits scientists were required to wear. One couldn't scratch an itchy nose or go to the bathroom, and fatigue set in quickly. Still, for Clements, it was a small price to pay for doing a job he loved, and one that rewarded him extremely well.

He worked in one of three adjacent high-containment laboratories situated in an incongruous building in the downtown area of a large American city. Lab A searched for a vaccine for the Ebola virus, Lab B was involved in ongoing research on H5N1, more commonly known as "Bird Flu". Lab C, however, Clements's domain, was involved in far more offensive research, that of developing future bioweapons.

A brilliant scientist, Clements was also a practical man. Seeing as *someone* would always accept the challenge of developing weaponized diseases for the US government, he saw no reason why that someone shouldn't be him. It paid a lot better than his university, too, where his groundbreaking research into virulent strains of respiratory diseases hadn't gone unnoticed by USAMRIID—the US Army Medical Research Institute of Infectious Diseases at Fort Detrick, Maryland. After what amounted on his part to feigned resistance that significantly increased the already huge salary he'd been offered, Clements resigned his post at the university, effective immediately.

For the past eight months, he'd been in charge of a small team of world class virologists, utilizing advanced cloning methods to isolate a variety of deadly viral pathogens, strengthening their potencies and improving their transmission capabilities. Recently, the team had developed vPx073, a mutant strain of smallpox that they had successfully spread among long-tailed macaques, a common proxy for humans during clinical research.

The monkeys had all died within a week. Even more satisfactory had been the fact that they'd become infectious in a matter of hours, and another group placed in a neighboring cage ten feet away died shortly after that as well. All indications were that vPx073 was even more deadly than the original disease, which had been responsible for killing more than three hundred million people over the course of the twentieth century.

Clements rose stiffly from his chair and arched his back. Being stooped over a microscope for the past three hours had left it aching. He unhooked the overhead hose attached to the respirator coupling at his waist, then crossed the room to the refrigerator where the new virus samples were being stored. Taking out the tray, he walked back to his lab station and hooked up again. The tubing supplied purified air into his "Blue Suit", and there were eight of them positioned around the lab.

He sat down again and concentrated on the task at hand, examining why this particular mutation had been so lethal. Like most sciences, virology involved a certain amount of trial and error, and he was keen to observe the molecular structure of this new batch.

He unscrewed the cap from the bijou bottle and used a pipette to first suck out, then squirt, a sample of the viral culture into a glass container. Sliding it under an electron microscope, through his visor he peered down at the distinctive dumbbell-shaped structure of the virions. He noted that the receptors on their envelopes matched exactly those the team had been looking for: receptors that could easily attach themselves to a human host cell, making the disease even more lethal than before.

For the next few hours, Clements concentrated hard, running a series of tests on the pathogen. Afterward, he sat back in his chair and marveled at his new creation.

Though he dealt with lethal viruses every day of his life, he couldn't help but feel a mixture of fear and awe. vPx073 was the ultimate "slate wiper". If released into the outside world, save for those perhaps working on oil rigs, nuclear submarines, or living in remote tribal areas, the entire planet would be wiped clean in a few short weeks.

Passed via airborne transmission, requiring only a tiny amount of particles to cause infection, and with a reproductive cycle of less than eight hours, it would spread like wildfire through the human population. Based on the macaque tests, Clements estimated it would kill its host within five to seven days of initial contact, other than perhaps a tiny percent of the population who would have a natural immunity.

He and his team would create an attenuated monoclonal antibody for the disease, one that could be administered quickly to a civilian population. Of course, this was all just academic research. The virus would never leave the confines of the lab, the work part of a new proliferation race taking place all over the world. As well as the US, there were now BSL-4 laboratories in Germany, Gabon, Sweden, Russia, South Africa, and Canada. Clements was sure there were many other undisclosed labs too, such as the one he worked in right now.

Finishing up, he put his instruments away, then carefully disposed of the waste materials. He untethered the tubing from his suit, hung up the nozzle, and walked over to a steel door at the far end of the lab. He punched a code into a small keypad and walked directly into the shower room, where he undertook a three-minute chemical shower, followed by a four-minute rinse.

Back in the changing room, he unzipped his suit from his left shoulder down to his right hip and stepped out of it. Hanging it up, he quickly got dressed and left the facility via a series of electronically-controlled doors requiring his fingerprint.

Out on the street, he walked back to the upmarket condo he was renting close by. He had a dinner date with a leggy brunette that evening, and wanted to get an hour's rest beforehand. Sally, with whom Clements had recently struck up a lunchtime conversation at a Starbucks, worked as an intern at a law firm nearby. This would be their third date, and he felt confident tonight would be the night he took her home.

***

Dr. Clements was correct about two things that day. After a pleasant dinner at a chic Japanese restaurant, he did indeed bed Sally, and the two had a most enjoyable night. In the morning, before heading to work, the two made passionate love in the shower again. After dressing, Clement called a cab, kissed Sally goodbye at his apartment door, and promised they would go out again soon. Through no fault of his own, or at least not intentionally, he never kept that promise.

The second thing Clements got right was that vPx073 killed its human host within the first week of initial exposure. Seventy-two hours later, he suffered from a high temperature and developed a mild rash on his face. The following day, the rash had progressed to lesions that became pus-filled with a sickly yellowish fluid that dripped from the sores.

By that time, he had been quarantined and interviewed by an emergency team of investigators who began the process of contact-tracing those who might have been exposed to the virus. Shortly after, Clements fell into a coma from which he never recovered.

Unfortunately for Sally, she didn't fare any better. Unfortunately for the world, nor did anyone else she came into contact with, including those at her busy law firm, many of whom either flew to or met with persons from other cities. In a short period of time, vPx073 was beyond containment.

Like happens with many of the accidental releases of pathogens at secure facilities such as the one he'd worked at, Clements had been unaware he had been infected until it was too late.

While returning from the refrigerator to his biosafety cabinet that afternoon, he'd unknowingly caught the air hose on the side of his chair, causing a two-inch tear in his suit underneath the hose coupling as he sat down. Although the positive pressure suit prevented viral material from entering small holes, ironically, the tear, being so close to the air intake hose, had blown vPx073 *into* his suit.

Though in and of itself a freak accident, statistically speaking it wasn't surprising. Since 2003, over a hundred labs experimenting with bioweapons had been cited by the CDC and USDA for serious safety and security failings. Just like Clements's research lab, many of these BSL-3 & -4 labs were located in the downtown areas of major US cities, such as New York, Atlanta, Kansas, and Seattle.

During that same timeframe, there had been dozens of reported cases of accidental lab-associated outbreaks across the world.

In 2004, an outbreak of SARS was traced back to lab workers at the National Institute of Virology in Beijing. In 2012, a researcher at San Francisco's VA medical center died after becoming exposed to the deadly *Neisseria meningitides* bacteria, and in 2015 a bioterror bacterium got out of a BSL-3 lab at the Tulane National Primate Research Center in New Orleans, presumed to have hitched a ride on a worker's clothing, and sickening several primates in outdoor cages in the process.

None of these outbreaks would have as dramatic an impact as the release of the viral contagion vPx073 into the world. A week in which the course of humanity took a huge step backward, and the world changed forever.

FROM THE AUTHOR

For sneak peaks, updates on new releases and bonus content, subscribe to my mailing list at www.mikesheridanbooks.com.

EASTWOOD, Book 2 in the NO DIRECTION HOME series is out now.

SPECIAL THANKS…

Goes to **Wmh Cheryl** (a proper prepper) for reviewing the book prior to release. Several of her suggestions made it into the story – and a few glaring errors hastily removed. Any remaining errors are all mine.

You can check her out on Facebook at **Off Grid Homestead Prepper**.